LIFE AS IT UNFOLDS

Clive Dev

THE ARREST

London city is looking very beautiful in the sunshine. It is a mild autumn day. The Giant Wheel in the far distance is rotating with the wind. It is a symbol of majesty, reflecting the richness of London's modern architecture; a continuation from the old to the new. The River Thames is catching the reflection of the buildings both old and the not so old; that are nestled on it's banks. Amongst this affluence is Clive's Poker Club, a gaming centre and casino of international repute. It is a massive two story building in the middle of the city centre with itsWell, own private car park. It is one of the well known

Strangers Inside

Story

Clive Dev

Chief Editor   Ashamole Clive

Leabharlanna Poiblí Chathair Baile Átha Cliath
Dublin City Public Libraries

Clive Dev

Disclaimer

This story is based on true events. However, the characters and the location has been changed to recreate this story as a book of fiction. The writers do not intend to hurt anyone's feelings but have attempted to highlight the various problems arising in the younger generation and the consequences of their action. No one should be subject to the events of this story in real life. Highlighting this is the purpose of this book. Any resemblance to any place, person or names is purely coincidental

highlights of the city. Tourists always have this location marked on their travel itinerary.

The club is loved by the locals as well. The entrance fee is quite modest. The plush interior and its opulence is a testimony to Clive's riches and the success of the club. Well, he is a millionaire-A very generous one. The poker club is his passion. He is a shrewd businessman with the casino being one among many of his 'small' scale ventures. This club has all the modern conveniences that are required to keep people from leaving. Oxygen is piped into the gaming area twenty-four hours a day and food and drinks are relatively inexpensive. Punters have an absolute certainty that they will win a big amount at least once. A jackpot to every player but, not everyday is a guarantee in this club. That was the shrewdness of Clive's business acumen.

The casino is circular in design. There are a few roulette table in the middle of the floor and people are supposed to be seated while playing. It gives a semblance of order and neatness to the place. The slot machines are very large and placed against the wall. They are connected to a chute in the wall. This chute pipes money in and out to and from the machines. The machines have a lot of space around it. It provides the punters with a sense of privacy. The machines in this place are always busy but no one is turned away because there is an overflow seating area with plush seats, bites of snacks, newspaper and historical gambling journals to while your time. The walls are covered with historical pictures of the city, photos of internationally reputed gamblers and the memoirs of the club's very own prodigies. One can glean the historical opulence from the past century by looking at these memoirs. The affluence of the people who visited this place in yester-years and yet the adaptation to accommodate the needs of the modern man in it's premises is obvious. As said earlier, no one is turned away.

Strangers Inside

The bar is a large space at the back wall. It is always busy and the bar tenders work for every penny they deserve. Yet, they all look very happy. They never smile through clenched teeth as most people in customer service do. Their smile actually reaches their eyes. Although many of the bar attendants are females, there is no lewdness in this place. There are quite a number of people in the bar. If you sit on the bar stool, you can see all the poker machines and the eager hands and the tense or not so tense bodies. Wait! Someone has just won a jackpot. You can hear the cheer go up from the far corner of the hall. Wow! This seems to be his lucky day. The man beside him is looking at him in envy. May be he is new to this place or probably a tourist and does not know that he will win eventually. The man who won the jackpot collected his prize money and left. Someone else is taking his place at the same machine. He is standing looking at the machine. Tension is visible all over his body. Looks like he is an Indian. Well, that is strange! Indians usually don't visit gambling dens.

They are very careful with their money. The sense of community in India is very strong and people go abroad to work so that they can earn enough money and then go back home. Most not all, of the tech guys work only for three or four months at a time and then go back to their own country. They may do another stint in a couple of years. Money is never enough isn't it. Oh look, he won a jackpot straightaway. Well, he doesn't seem to be celebrating. Wonder what is wrong and what is going through his head?

Cheenu is in another world completely. He is oblivious to the amount of money that he has won. He continues to play. The noises coming from all the other machines are soothing him as well. It is like a sweet melody to his ears. He won a small jackpot again and slowly he is becoming aware of his win. But his face is screwed in bitterness. This is not a timely win. A little bit too late!

Had he won even a fraction of this a few days ago; he would not be in the situation he is in now. He hopes that he does not have to face the consequences for his actions. He smiles to himself bitterly. "That is fooling himself" he thinks. Every one has to pay for their actions good or bad. Karma is inescapable. As his dad always says-"One who eats salt has to drink water". Hope it is not soon though. Hope he is able to escape. He is not happy with what he has done and yet he feels no remorse. The winning from the machine is making him more feverish and irritated.

Suddenly Cheenu becomes very alert. Realization dawns on him slowly that his machine is the only one making all the noise. None of the other machines are being operated. The only noise coming from those machines is the usual music of inactivity. Something is not quite right. He turns his head slightly. The other machines are vacant. The people who were using those slots were not there any more. That is not the usual pattern for this place. Suddenly a shiver runs down his spine. He begins to perspire. He needs to get out. He is suffocating in here. The oxygen coming through the pipes is not enough anymore. A voice which conveys authority and intent comes from behind him. "This is the police. Kneel down on the floor with your hands behind you and don't turn around".

Cheenu hesitates. He tries to reach his back-pocket but one of the officer shoots him in the leg. Detective Dev who is heading the team of officers have come to arrest Cheenu on the suspicion of a dreadful crime. Cheenu falls to the floor howling in pain and he rubs his blood soaked knee. Officer Dev appears within his line of vision. Dev still has his gun pointed at Cheenu and is anticipating his next move. A few gasps come from the crowd behind him. Two deputies turn around to calm the people at the back. They look at them and signal them to keep quiet. Detective Dev speaks to Cheenu "Cheenu put your hands behind your back. You have no way to escape".

Cheenu slowly places his hand behind his back. Brenda who is Dev's assistant comes forward and handcuffs Cheenu.

Cheenu is assisted to get up by one of the deputies. He had moved forward to assist Brenda. Cheenu again cries out in pain. He is now turned away from the wall and facing the centre of the room. He realises that the punters have all gone. Only the casino staff were the witness to the scene and they look horrified. Two deputies assist him to walk out through the back door. Detective Dev follows their progress with his eyes all the way to the door. He then turns around and addresses the crowd. "Sorry for all the commotion folks! It is fine now and you can continue with your work. Thank you for your co-operation". He then walks out with his assistant.

Cheenu on walking out with the assistants is blinded by the sudden light outside. He gasps when he sees the campus surrounded by the police with their flash lights turned on. The police were just a silhouette in the darkness beyond the perimeter of light. The rest of the world was pitched in darkness. Winter in the northern hemisphere-darker evenings and darker mornings. It adds to a person's sense of desperation. Slowly his eyes adjust to the bright light. He now knows that he could not have escaped this lot even if he were able to get out to the door. He was only an ordinary man not an athlete, gangster or a member of the mafia.

The place was crawling with the police. Cheenu is directed with his head bent over into the back passenger seat of the patrol car. The deputy enters the driver's side and sits in the seat. He keeps a careful eye on Cheenu. Another deputy enters and sits in the front passenger seat. Once they get the signal from Detective Dev, the car drives away.

Detective Dev turns around to his deputies and gives them some orders. He also gets into his car. Assistant Brenda joins him in the car and they drive off. Now the two cars are speeding with full sirens blaring to the police station. They take the Bypass route to avoid general traffic. Inside the car, Brenda is entering notes into her laptop. Dev keeps his eyes on the road. Brenda finishes writing her notes in a few moments. Dev comments "This is why I like working with you Brenda" You are always very organised, meticulous and up to date with your work." Brenda looked at Dev and smiled. She came back with a cheeky retort "Well I have to keep up with my senior." Dev smiled to himself. The car reached the police headquarters. The vehicle which had transported Cheenu has also just pulled up. They get him out of the transport vehicle and walk him into the building.

The deputies bring Cheenu to one of the interrogation rooms and sit him down on the chair. They released the handcuffs and leave the room. A plastic glass filled with water is kept on the table. The room has another chair on the other side of the table. There is an inbuilt tape recorder on the table which is fixed. The two corner cameras on the ceiling of the room are actively capturing the scene below. The deputies are waiting in the observation room. Their eyes are fixed on Cheenu who picks up the glass of water and drinks it. He looks around the room and then at his knee. It is still bleeding but very slightly. He then leans his head back on the chair and closes his eyes. The pain is bearable if he does not move it. Detective Dev is a good shot. He did not want the bullet to lodge in his knees. The bullet just scraped his skin and probably lodged itself somewhere in the wall of the casino. After some time, he hears the door open again and opens his eyes. Two paramedics walk in to the room to provide first aid to Cheenu. They are handling him very gently yet the pain in his knees is horrible. He smiles bitterly to himself. "You inflicted this on your own self." But he also justified to himself, 'What was I supposed to do though?' Once the paramedics leave, Detective

Dev and Assistant Brenda walk into the room. A deputy brings an extra chair for Brenda. She has a note pad and pen in her hand.

Dev switched on the tape recorder and did a sound check. He rewinded the machine and listened to his own voice. He is satisfied that the tape recorder is functioning well. He then speaks into the microphone. "Date: 11/11/2017 Time: 19:30 Detective Dev and Assistant Detective Brenda interrogating Mr. Cheenu regarding the double murder of baby Aishwarya and Mrs. Nayagam."

The tape-recorder remains turned on and Dev looked up at Cheenu. "Cheenu you are under arrest on suspicion of the double murder of baby Aishwarya and Mrs. Nayagam. You do not have to say anything but it may harm your defense if you do not mention when questioned something which you later rely on in court. Anything you do say may be given in evidence" Dev continued after a pause

"Do you understand this?" Cheenu replied "Yes" to the question. Dev added, "You also have the right to a lawyer who you can contact once we have processed your papers. Your entitlements are written on that laminated frame in the wall. Do you understand English?" Cheenu nodded his head in affirmation.

Dev said to him, "You can also see the police interview 'Code of Conduct' if you wish. Is it okay to proceed?" Cheenu again replied "Yes". Dev asked him his country of birth. He added that they knew his local address. Cheenu replied that he was from Chennai in India. Dev's next question was, 'When did you emigrate to London?' Cheenu softly said. "I completed my studies in IIT Chennai and then came to London to work three years ago." Dev asked Cheenu if he had any friends or relatives. "Do you wish to inform someone that you are in the Police station?" Cheenu answered in the negative to both questions.

Dev looked at his checklist on the interrogation form, "Do you have a lawyer?" Cheenu said that he did not have one. Dev advised him that Cheenu had the right to free counsel. There were three options. The first one was his own lawyer which he did not have. The second option was the 'duty solicitor' who was present in the building and the third option was legal advice. "Do you want to avail of any of the two suggestions?" Cheenu replied, "Yes, I would like to avail of legal advice". Dev informed him that Cheenu will be processed now and meanwhile they will organise a Defense Solicitor for him. Dev asked him. "Do you know what processing means?" Cheenu who had never been to a police station ever before in his life had no clue. Dev supplied the meaning of processing. "One of the deputies will take your photographs and swab you for DNA evidence. Then you will be brought to a cell to wait for legal advice. Is that clear?' Cheenu replied that he understood. Detective Dev now spoke into the tape-recorder. "The interview is terminated as the suspect has requested for Legal Advice. Time: 20:00 Date: 11/11/2017". Dev indicated to Brenda who got up from her chair and opened the door of the interrogation room. Two deputies walked in and Dev and Brenda walked out.

The deputies helped Cheenu up from the chair and brought him to the roomAll right of the Custody Officer. Here he was stood against a wall and photographed from three angles-Front, left and right. Then his mouth and the skin of his arms were swabbed. He was then brought to a Custody Suite. This suite is a temporary hold up area for suspects and is furnished with a bed, pillow and an overhead light. One of the deputy addressed Cheenu and informed him that his dinner will be brought to him shortly. Then they left the room and locked it behind them. They observed him from the outside for a short while. Cheenu lay down in the bed with his face covered with his hands. The deputies left the corridor after some time.

Meanwhile Assistant Brenda rang the 'Defense Solicitor Call Centre'. She came off the phone and informed Dev that the defense lawyer had spoken to Cheenu on another line. "The solicitor has given us an appointment for 10 am in the morning." Dev shrugged his shoulders "All right, keep him safe and out of trouble. I will be back tomorrow morning". He suggested to Brenda that she should leave as well once the night staff come on duty. Brenda answered "Good night Detective Dev. I have some more paper work to do. I will leave after that." Dev said good night and left. And he walked out the door.

He got into his car and drove by the River Thames. It was late at night, but the traffic in London was very much alive and active. The tail lights of the cars looked like the glowing red feet of a millipede in the darkness. All in a neat order, moving at the same time in a synchronised fashion in response to the traffic lights. He did not mind the busyness at this time of the night. The view of the Millennium bridge and the London skyline gave him a sense of peace and serenity. He opened the window and the cool breeze enveloped him. It is a cold evening. He whistled softly to himself. He is happy with the day's work and is looking forward to the night ahead.

The next morning, Dev drives to work and as usual prepares his first mug of brew. He likes it strong and sweet. He sighs with satisfaction and sits down at his table to begin his work. After some time Assistant Brenda knocked at the door. She popped her head inside the door wished him good morning. "It is 0930. Do you want to go for breakfast before the defense solicitor arrives?" Dev looked at the time and rolled his eyes up to the heavens. "We might as well. Where does the time go?" Dev asked her if she knew the name of the solicitor who was coming in the morning. "Solicitor John Noel. I have never worked with him before. Hope he is a sensible person," Brenda answered. Dev and Brenda walked in to the local Deli. There they ordered a coffee and a bowl of porridge each and sat down in the lounge. They ate their breakfast in peace and got up to go. The defense lawyer was waiting in the visiting room. Detective Dev welcomed him and escorted him into the interview room. Brenda walked over to the general office and instructed the deputies to bring Cheenu to the interview room.

Solicitor John Noel was seated on a chair behind the table in the interview room. Cheenu walked in. On seeing him come in the door, John stood up and extended his hand to Cheenu. "Hello Cheenu, my name is John Noel. I am a solicitor from the Defense Solicitor call centre. I spoke to you last night. Please take a seat. Are you happy to proceed?" Cheenu shook John's hand and sat down on the chair across from him. John continued "I will be your legal advice for the case. Just to make you aware that you can also pay for an independent legal advice other than myself. Do you want to do that?" Cheenu said that he didn't want to do so. John rubbed his hands together to counteract the cold in the room. "All right then. Cheenu! Let me begin by advising you that during the interrogation, if you are unsure, look at me before answering the question from the police officers. If I nod then you give the answer and if I stay quiet then don't answer the question. Is that understood?" Cheenu nodded his head in response. John further added, "I have briefed myself with your file. But I want to hear your version. Please tell me your side of the story."

THE INTERROGATION

Meanwhile, Brenda and Dev are in their office working away on preparing for the interrogation. Sometime later, Solicitor John walked into their office and called out. "Hello may I come in?" Dev looked up at him and smiled. "You are already in." John looked at him sheepishly. "Yes, well, Of course. Anyway, if you are ready to interrogate, my client is ready and willing to be interrogated."

Detective Dev looked at Brenda who nodded her head. Then Dev looked up at John and replied, "Okay we are ready. If you don't mind, can you please walk your client up to the interrogation room? One of the deputies will guide you". "Okay thanks" replied John and walked away. Dev looked up at Brenda and rolled his eyes. Brenda smiled at him in response. Dev explained the method to Brenda, "Okay, this is the strategy. We are going to be tough. I can assume that the suspect has been coached well. There will be loads of interruptions and interference but we cannot slacken the pace. Is that understood?" Brenda who was cognisant of her boss' style of working was amused. There will be no two ways about it. "Yes, Dev."

She gathered her files while Dev walked out. Brenda followed him quickly and they both walked to the interrogation room. John and Cheenu were seated on one side. Dev and Brenda took the two chairs across from them. Dev switched on the tape recorder and did a sound check. He rewinded the tape and listened to his own voice. He is satisfied that the tape recorder is functioning well. He then spoke into the microphone. "Date 12/11/2017 Time 10:30 Interrogation of Mr. Cheenu by Detective Dev and Assistant Brenda in the presence of the counsel John Noel." Dev now looked at Cheenu. "Cheenu, you have been advised of your rights. Do you wish to hear them again?" Cheenu nodded his head. Dev was annoyed. "You have to speak up. We need to record everything."

Cheenu now said, "Yes" Dev continued, "You can request for a break if you wish to speak to your counsel in private. You can also request for bathroom breaks and refreshments break. We anticipate your co-operation in this interrogation. Is that okay?" Cheenu said, "Yes" out aloud this time.

Dev looked at him kindly, "Tell us a little bit about yourself." Cheenu replied, "My name is Cheenu and I come from Chennai, India. I have a degree in Technology and straight after College, I got recruited through campus interview and arrived here. I have no family here." Cheenu stopped speaking." Dev asked him," Where do you work and what is your salary?" Cheenu replied that he worked with Messers ECC Ltd. And the salary was 8000 pounds. Dev asked him, "Do you have any friends here?" Cheenu sighed "No, I only know my office colleagues." Dev asked him, "Do you have a girlfriend?" Cheenu said that he had no girlfriend. Dev looked at his file and looked up at Cheenu. "What do you do in your free time?" Cheenu replied that he worked during the day and in the evenings he stayed at home. Dev looked at him for long and then asked, "Do you go out?" Cheenu replied that he went out to the local park. Dev next wanted to know, "What do you do during the weekend?" Cheenu replied, "I go out to visit tourist attractions."

Dev wanted to know if he went alone. Cheenu replied, "Initially, I used to go out with my colleagues who were as new as me. Now I go on my own." Dev asked him if he ever gambled. Cheenu looked at John who nodded his head. Cheenu looked at Dev and said, "Yes sometimes." Dev asked him, "Did you ever win anything?" Cheenu replied that he had once before and then last night. Dev wanted to know if Cheenu had any outstanding debts? Cheenu looked at John who stayed quiet. Cheenu said to Dev, "No" Dev looked at Cheenu intently. "Cheenu, you might as well know that hiding any fact is a crime. I am sure that your solicitor has advised you of that?" Dev glared at John. Cheenu nodded. Dev continued, "And that if we have arrested you on suspicion, it is not mere suspicion. We have done our homework very well. You are seventy-five thousand pounds in debt. There is no bank transaction in your account apart from your salary coming in and your rent going out. You withdraw the rest of the money from your account and you gamble everyday. The banks have declared against furnishing you with any loan. Three of your loan applications each to a different bank to the value of eighty-thousand has been rejected. All your loans are from Loan sharks and now they are after you for their money."

Cheenu sat quietly. There was no reaction from him. He did not even look at his counsel. Dev eyed Brenda who kept her note pad face down and poured some water for Cheenu. He gulped it down. Dev keeps looking at him intently. "So tell me how did you do this?" Cheenu looked at Dev in desperation. John got the feeling that Cheenu is about to confess. John keeps his hand on Cheenu's shoulder who in turn remains quiet. John interjected, "My client needs a bathroom break. If you don't mind, I will escort him to the toilet." Dev sighed, "Okay, no problem. Take your time." Dev spoke into the microphone. "Interrogation temporarily suspended for a bathroom break. Time 12:30 Date 12/11/2017."

John and Cheenu walked out of the door and Dev looked at Brenda in exasperation. He picked up a sheet of paper and crumpled it. He threw it viciously into the waste paper basket in the corner of the room. "He was about to break. Pity, the lawyer took him away." Brenda quietly states that John is doing his job. Dev replied, "I know but that is the problem. He is a very good defense lawyer. Cheenu is lucky that he got the very best of the defense solicitors. John and Cheenu entered the room. Cheenu's steps are much more confident this time. Dev switched on the tape recorder and did a sound check. He rewinded the tape and listened to his own voice. He is satisfied that the tape recorder is functioning well. He then spoke into the microphone. "Date 12/11/2017 Time 13:00 Interrogation continued of Mr. Cheenu by Detective Dev and Assistant Brenda in the presence of the counsel John Noel". Dev tries to assess Cheenu's behaviour. It is evident that the defense lawyer has boosted his confidence. Dev takes another approach. He opens his file and he shows the photo of baby Aishwarya and asks Cheenu. "Do you know this baby?" Cheenu replied, "Yes". Dev felt a small amount of hope, "How do you know this baby?"

Cheenu's memory goes back to his initial days in London.

The office of messers ECC Ltd. Company is a huge building along the sea coast. The security is at the gate in his starched uniform. As people walk into the building, they enter a very large foyer with high ceiling hung with expensive chandeliers. There is a reception desk in the corner where a receptionist who is well trained in customer service is answering telephone calls with a smile. She terminates the phone call and looked up at the person standing on the other side of the counter. He is a tall young man approximately 5'11" and is dark and handsome. She asked him politely "May I help you sir?

Cheenu replied enthusiastically, "Hi, my name is Cheenu and I am here to join as a Customs relations Officer". The receptionist smiled happily, "Hello Cheenu, my name is Emily and I am the receptionist here. So you are the one who is going to join me in this office? Nice to meet you." Emily offered her hand in welcome. Cheenu shook her hands with enthusiasm. "Nice to meet you as well." Emily replied apologetically, "I would like to speak to you more but first you have to meet the person from Human Resources. If you don't mind having a seat in the foyer, I will ring HR. Someone will come down and set you up in the system." Cheenu acknowledged Emily's explanation. "Okay, thanks". He took a seat in the foyer and began to read the newspaper kept at the table. The receptionist picked up the hand set and dialled a number.

A few days later, Cheenu was sitting in the office canteen. He is sitting on his own at a table deep in thought. He is having the lunch that was served in the canteen when someone walked up to him. "Hi, do you mind if I join you? Cheenu looked up in surprise. "Oh no, not at all. Please." He pointed to the seat beside him. This man placed his lunch plate at the table and sat down beside him. He offered his hand to Cheenu. "My name is Venkat. I work in the sales section." Cheenu shook his hand. "My name is Cheenu. I work in Customer relation. I am new here. What about you?" Venkat replied "No I am not new. You have not seen me around because I went home on vacation. I arrived only last week with my new bride." Cheenu was delighted, "Wow, congratulations. What is your wife's name?" Venkat happily supplied the information, "Her name is Priya. Are you married?" Cheenu smiled, "No I am not. I have finished my education recently. I am not in any rush to get married." Venkat asked him, "Where do you live?" Cheenu said that he lived in a small hotel near by. It was very expensive. But there is a place to sleep. "What about you?"

Venkat said that initially he did the same as Cheenu. "But when I knew that I was going home to get married, I moved into a new house. I have to go back to work now but when we meet next time, we can make arrangements for you to visit us at home. My wife's cooking is great. Cheenu was grateful, "Thank you so much. Even if it was not great; I will eat anything that comes from our cuisine and is homemade." Venkat and Cheenu share a laugh at the thought. Venkat waved goodbye and walked away. Cheenu looked at his food and pushed it away

with distaste. Suddenly he felt very lonely.
By the evening he was back to normal
But the long evening is now stretching
ahead of him.   He decided to take a
walk. He saw Clive's poker club in the
centre of the town. The club looked very
posh. Curiosity took the better of him
and he began to walk to the club. He
approached the counter and bought coins
worth twenty-five Pounds. He played for
a good while. His stack came down to
four pounds. It then became zero and he
went home with disappointment.

Cheenu went back to work the next day.
He cleared his desk and went for lunch.
Once he had finished his lunch, he went
out for a smoke and then back to work
again. After work,   the empty evening
was again yawning in front of him. He
again took a walk and found himself in
front of the casino. He walked in.

Life now takes this pattern for Cheenu.
He works during the day and goes to the
casino in the evening. One day in the

evening, Cheenu goes to one of the slot machines and plays furiously. He has bought coins for a thousand pounds and now his stack of coins is down to four hundred pounds. He goes out for some fresh air. There are other people who are smoking in the area. Cheenu brings his cigarette case out and selects a cigarette. He searches his pocket for a lighter and does not find one. He walks to the nearest person who is a female. "May I borrow your lighter please?"The girl replied, "Yes of course" and handed him the lighter. Cheenu lit his cigarette and took a puff. Meanwhile the girl looked him up and down. Cheenu handed the lighter back with a thanks and a smile. The girl acknowledged his thanks with a smile. Both of them smoke their cigarettes in silence. Next the girl finished her smoke and walked back into the casino. Suddenly Cheenu's phone vibrates in his pocket.

He lifts the phone out of his pocket, looked at the caller id and answered. "Hello mum, how are you?" Cheenu's mother on other end. "I am good. How are you son ?" Cheenu replied "I am good mum. I have met a person from our state and he is very good." His mother was happy to hear that, "I am delighted to hear that. I wanted to hear your voice before I went to bed. I know that it is not even dinner time for you yet. Eat properly and sleep well." Cheenu replied, "I will mother. Good night." His mother disconnected the line, "Good night my child." Cheenu hangs up the phone and looks miserable and deep in thought. He went back inside to continue his game. He kept playing. The girl is on the slot beside him. Suddenly his machine gives a loud beep. He has won a jack pot of five hundred pounds and he gives a joyful shout.

Cheenu shouted with joy, "Oh wow! I have won five hundred pounds. That is cool." The girl looked at him happily. "Wow, congratulations. You got your lucky break." Cheenu responded, "Thanks. My name is Cheenu. The girl said, "My name is Hema" Cheenu acknowledged her name, "Hi Hema, it has been a while since I have won anything." Hema said, "Yes, I have seen you many times here. Cheenu remarked, "That means you are a regular here as well?" Hema said, "Yes, I come sometimes. I like to play for fun."

Cheenu responded happily, "Great I will have company from now on. What do you say? Shall we go out and celebrate the dual victory?" Hema was curious, "Dual victory?" Cheenu is now embarrassed. He just took it for granted that this girl will accept his friendship. He finished lamely, "Well, me winning the jackpot and you becoming my friend." Hema understood his hesitation, "Why not? Let's go."

Cheenu and Hema walked to the concierge who handed them their coats. Cheenu helped Hema into her court and then he put on his own jacket. Together they walked out of the building into the night air. They talked as they walked along the canal and reached a pub. The pub was very cosy and welcoming. There was a large fire roaring in the ancient fireplace in the corner. The sound of music was emanating from a juke box. 1980 hits were belting out of the music system. Cheenu and Hema sat in a corner table and checked the drinks menu. Cheenu went to the bar to place their order. Once seated, they were deep in conversation and were enjoying themselves. They walked out of the pub after a few hours.

Cheenu was sitting with his laptop on his lap. He was working furiously but kept checking the clock every five minutes. His room mate was lying down on the couch and listening to the native music of his country. Cheenu looked up at his room mate. "Hey Mukil, can you give me a thousand Pound please. I will return it you on pay-day" Mukil replied, "Sorry Cheenu, I have only five hundred pounds with me. Can you organise the rest?" Cheenu was not pleased but he agreed. "Okay thanks. I will try else where."

Once Mukil handed him the money, he went outside to make a phone-call to his other roommate. "Sanjay, I need some money. I will pay you back when I get my salary. I am going out on a date". Sanjay was envious, "You lucky fellow. Go on enjoy. Come to my office and collect the money." Cheenu thanked him and hung up the phone. He got ready and went out to collect the money from his friend. Then, he walked up to meet Hema at the bus stop. "Hi, how was your day?" Hema pulled a face. "Same as usual."

Cheenu consoled her. "Don't worry. We will hit the jackpot one day and our lives will change. I will share the money with you." Hema looked at him indulgently but he can see that she is upset. "Hey what's wrong?" he asked. Hema said that her mother rang her today. "She asked me to come and stay with her for a while." Cheenu had a worried expression on his face, "Is she all right?" Hema quickly reassured him, "Oh she is fine but she got divorced after twenty-five years of marriage. Her and my dad always behaved as if they were made for each other. Now they can't stand each other. Life is so unpredictable. Cheenu hugged her and comforted her. "I am so sorry Hema. Come on; let's go and get some drinks. That might relax you." Together they walked to Clive's Poker club. They bought a few drinks and began to play on their individual machines. They played with gusto and continuously with the exception of a few smoking breaks and to replenish their drinks. Life looked very beautiful at the time. No cares, no worries. Nobody to answer to. Only if it always remained the same.....

Hema is in her bed lying down and reading a magazine. Cheenu is out in the kitchen and making coffee. He looked very comfortable in this kitchen. He brings the two coffee mugs out to the drawing table. He sets it there and sits down on the couch. And calls out, "Hema! Coffee is ready." Hema lifted up her head from the pillow and called back with a smile in her voice, "Coming out". She got up from her bed, admired herself in the mirror and went to the ensuite. She came out in a few minutes and joined Cheenu at the living room table. "Thanks for the coffee Cheenu. Did you sleep well last night? The couch is not that comfortable."

Cheenu replied, "No, I slept very well. Thanks for accommodating me. I was way out of my usual tolerance level for alcohol." Hema laughed, "You are welcome. It was funny to see you weaving across the road in front of oncoming cars. Half of the time, I was terrified." Hema took a sip from her mug and sighed pleasantly. "lovely coffee. Cheenu smiled, "When are you leaving? Hema said that she was leaving the next day. "I have booked the tickets. I just need to hand over the keys to the land lord." Cheenu asked her if she needed any help from him? Hema answered affectionately, "No thanks Cheenu. You mind yourself."

She looked around the room and up at the ceiling and then focused her gaze on him. "You know I will miss this house and you a lot." Cheenu said quietly, "Me too. But at-least your mother will be happy." Hema lamented her status of being an only child. "Yeah I know. I don't know if I will be ever back. She sounded very vulnerable on the phone. You know I never regretted not having siblings except for now. If I had brothers and sisters, she could have divided her time equally amongst us all. Slowly she would have gained her confidence and eventually her independence and we could have got on with our lives once more. I know that I sound selfish but parents expect us not to hang around them for ever. They want us to get on with our lives and be happy." Cheenu said with a huge relief, "Yeah I know. I have no siblings thank God. My parents are well off and still together so they don't rely on me which is good." Hema teased him, "I am sure you were the spoilt one" Cheenu grinned, "Yep, that's me." He beat his chest like a bear. Hema laughed out aloud. He was so funny.

Clive Dev

Cheenu got up to go and Hema sat up
from her chair as well. She hugged him
squeezing hard. "Mind yourself. I am
going to miss you so much." Cheenu bid
farewell to her and walked out of Hema's
apartment. He gets a phone-call on his
mobile from his friend Venkat. "Hey
Cheenu, where are you? Don't forget our
lunch appointment for this afternoon.

Cheenu laughed, "No definitely not. I am
looking forward to it" and hung up the
mobile. Around lunch time, Cheenu
arrived at Venkat's house and knocked on
the door. Venkat opened the door and
invited Cheenu to come in. "Come in
Cheenu. How are you?" He then looked
in the direction of the kitchen, "Priya,
Cheenu is here." Priya came out to the
living room. She is heavily pregnant and
has Symphysis Pubis Dysfunction-a
problem of the muscles and joints during
pregnancy. It resolves after the baby is
born. Venkat turned to look at the sound
of his wife shuffling in. "Hello brother.
Please come in and take a seat." Cheenu
acknowledged the progress of her

pregnancy, "Hello sister, how are you? Looks like baby is due any-day. The pain of your hip looks even worse than the last time I saw you."

Priya smiled indulgently at his consideration, "Yes it is getting more worse everyday. But it will be over very soon now. We can't wait to see our baby. Don't know if it is boy or a girl..." She stopped speaking in mid-stride and was embarrassed, "Anyway please make yourself comfortable. I will bring you both something to drink." Venkat and Cheenu sat down on the couch. Cheenu looked around the house. It was very tastefully decorated. Every time he visits, there will be something new added to the décor. This time it is the crochet pattern hangings on the door. Large green mango leaves with small white and yellow mango flowers-a symbol of prosperity. Each leaf and bloom has been painstakingly, patiently and lovingly made. It reminded him of his own home. His mother is an expert at homemaking and had decorated their house with artistic, simple stuff that gives the house a sense of home. Cheenu said to Venkat, "Your wife has great skills. She has decorated the house so beautifully. You are very blessed." Venkat looked in the direction of the kitchen, "Yes I know. She has changed my life around. It will only get better with the baby's arrival. How is your mother Cheenu?"

Cheenu replied, "She is fine. She misses me a lot and wants me to visit.Venkat observed quietly, "You have not gone back since you first arrived to London." Cheenu said, "No, I have not. But I don't know when I am going to go." Venkat said, "I think you are worried about saying goodbye to her again but I know from experience that you will feel better once you have seen her. He then continued with a playful smile on his lips. 'OR Are you afraid that she will marry you off to someone you don't know? I would like to think that even our parents have moved beyond that." Cheenu just laughs. 'I say it is a bit of both. My parents will respect my wishes but they will expect me to settle down soon. I am not ready to settle down just yet." Just then Priya walked out into the living room with two glasses of home made fruit juice and hands a glass each to Cheenu and to her husband. 'You better get married soon brother. I have no females for company." Cheenu laughed, "Okay sister, your wish is my command," Venkat joined in the laughter as well. Priya made a face at her husband, "Enjoy the juice. Lunch will be ready in ten minutes." Venkat reassured her, "Take your time Priya. We have to discuss a few issues anyway and the juice will keep us going."

Cheenu takes a sip of the juice. He looks up at Priya: 'Sister, your culinary skills are just getting better and better. I can't wait to taste lunch. I will happily become your Guinea Pig. Let me know when you are trying out new recipes." Priya laughed and slowly walked back into the kitchen.

THE UNHAPPY MISTRESS

There is a row of posh houses beside the River Thames. Cheenu entered the gates of one of the houses. He is escorted by the security to the front door. Here he is handed over to and escorted by another man who looked like a dodgy character. A man was sitting on a rocking chair. Across from him, another man was tied to the post. Few men are torturing him with their fists. You can sense the flesh under the skin being pounded and bruised just like a piece of steak. Cheenu can hear the heart rendering scream come for inside the house. His heart sinks.

The voice from inside the house begs, "Please let me go boss. I will return your money within the week". Cheenu's heart sinks even further. Another person who has probably borrowed a large sum. He gathers his courage and walks into the room. The voice further pleads "I have already paid you so much money." The mafia boss roars out in anger "Yeah! You have paid, but that may not be enough. I charge less interest. But even a small interest builds up to a huge amount overtime. You came to me after being rejected everywhere else. Do you know of anyone else who will give you a low interest rate and lots of time? Call someone, do something. If you don't pay the money back by this evening, I will not do anything to you but I will hurt your family."

He instructed his men to haul him up from the floor and drop him to wherever he wanted to go. He turned back and sees Cheenu, "Ah Cheenu. You are here at last. We are treating you mildly because you are an educated fellow and I would like to believe that you have more sense. I think you also need a taste of my treatment."

Cheenu replies meekly, "No boss. I have got some money with me now. I will repay the rest very soon." The man is

Clive Dev

slightly appeased "Go then and see the accountant. Find out how much you owe me." He further added, "Cheenu, I have heard about you. My men have told me that you gamble a lot. You are an educated man. You should have more sense than that. Gambling causes you to lose your self respect and also everything that you possess. She is a very hard to please mistress. Be careful." Meanwhile the gangster's men have tied up the man who was screaming for his life and hauled him into the van.

Mafia boss turns to his men: Don't let him go till you have recovered all of what he owes us." He turns back again to Cheenu. "My men are very unpredictable in their behaviour. They are not kind everyday. If you want to avoid his fate, you better return the money soon. I hope you understand that." Cheenu nods his head and walks to the office room.

Cheenu is in his office busy at work . His phone rings, It is a call from Venkat. Cheenu answers, "Hello Venkat, how are you." Venkat speaks in a very elated voice, "Cheenu, Priya gave birth to a baby girl. I have become a father now." Cheenu is thrilled "Congratulations. Venkat. How is Priya?" Venkat replies with pride, "She is a bit tired but in great form. They are both asleep at present. Look I am going to get off the phone. I need to make a few more phone calls." Cheenu promises him that he will visit in the evening. Cheenu smiles to himself and hangs up the phone.

Cheenu goes to the hospital in the evening with a gift bag. The hospital corridors are very busy. He goes to the reception and enquires about Priya. He is directed to the top floor. He reaches in front of the correct room and knocks on the door. Venkat opens the door and welcomes Cheenu in. Priya is asleep in bed with the baby behind the curtain. Priya's mother, Venkat's mother-in-law is sitting on a chair beside her daughter's bed. Cheenu greets everyone and he hands over the gift bag to Venkat. Venkat thanks him and hands over the bag to the mother-in-law who places it in a corner. Venkat introduces Cheenu to his mother-in-law. "Mother, this is my colleague Cheenu." And then to Cheenu, "Cheenu this is my mother-in-law. Have a seat, I am going to the canteen while you both are chatting." "Okay Venkat, see you soon" said Cheenu.

Cheenu began to speak to the elderly lady, "Hello mother, how are you?" Mrs. Nayagam replied, "I am fine Cheenu, how are you? It is good to see that my daughter and Son-in-law have so many friends." Cheenu said, "I am fine mother. You are correct. It is difficult to survive without friends when you are in another country. How is everything for you here? She says that it is all good except for the cold which is unbearable. Just then Priya wakes up from her sleep. She sits up and pulls the curtain. "Hello sister, congratulations. How are you?" he asked. Priya looked up at him and smiled a happy but tired smile. "Thanks brother." Priya hands the baby over to Cheenu who holds her tenderly. He touches her face and welcomes her to the world. "Welcome to our world Sweetie."

Venkat arrived back from the canteen with coffee and offered it to everyone in the room but Cheenu declined. Priya thanks him for the gifts and insists to him to drink coffee however he declines adamantly. "Thank you both, but I have to be somewhere else urgently. I will call you later Venkat". Cheenu looked at Priya's mother and smiles affectionately, and said "Mother, I will see you again soon"

He then leaves the room and goes out into the corridor. Once he reaches the main road he gets into a taxi and urges the taxi driver to get to Clive's poker club urgently. He gets out at the poker club and goes past the concierge in a hurry. The concierge also waves him in as Cheenu is a frequent visitor there. He goes and starts playing on a machine. His hands are moving at great speed. All the time he is mumbling to himself and silently urging the machine to hand him large sums of money as jackpot. "Come on— don't be so mean. I have been playing for so long but you are not giving me anything. I need something big." Beside him a drunken man is on another machine and he is mumbling to himself. "Aw, come on (hick) I have lost everything (hick). This is my last coin. Give something to me now (Hick)."

Cheenu gets more frustrated hearing this and he walks out to the smoking area irritatedly. He begins to smoke and he looks at a piece of paper that he took out from his pocket. He is calculating something and mumbling to himself. There is a frenzy in his behaviour. He is agitated.

Next day, he is back to his office and is engrossed in his work. The others are also working; but there is a calmness around them whereas, Cheenu looks frustrated. There is an air of tension in his personal work space. He had received a new text from the loan shark this morning and to put it mildly, it was a very nasty text.

In the evening, Cheenu went back to the poker club again. He was high on alcohol and calculating the money owed by him which he had written on a piece of paper. He was definite that it probably has increased another ten percent by now. All he can think about is the loan shark. Then he becomes upset again. He walks to the poker machine and begins to play. He is very feverish and visibly frustrated. He is shaking, shivering and mumbling to himself. "I will get you. I will get you one day."

Cheenu is agitated and he needs a smoke so he goes out into the smoking area at the edge of the road. He sees that the prostitutes are displaying their ware to potential customers. One of the prostitutes comes near Cheenu and enquires if he was interested in spending time with her. "Hi baby! How are you? Ah you don't look very happy do you? Shall we go for a bite to eat and some fun afterwards? I won't charge you much." Cheenu does not pay any attention.

Some other prostitutes are having an argument with a potential customer over the going rate. She shouts at him and he insults her. She insults him in return and goes away. She turns around and sees Cheenu. She smiles coquettishly and gives him a flying kiss. She walks away and a car approaches her. The car driver opens the window and signals her to come nearer. She goes over to the driver and after some discussion she gets into the car and he drives away.

Cheenu observes all of this but he is not paying attention. His mind is elsewhere.

He takes out his mobile phone from his pocket and calls someone.

NAMING CEREMONY

Venkat has invited everyone to his house to the naming ceremony of his daughter. He and Priya are standing at the doorway and welcoming everyone. Priya's mother is sitting on the sofa in the middle of the room with the baby asleep in her arms. They are all dressed in their traditional finery. The baby is wearing a beautiful colorful frock which Priya's mother had brought over from India. It is customary that the maternal uncle brings the biggest gift for his niece or nephew. Priya's mother brought it to her on behalf of her son. It is a predominant aspect of culture anywhere in India. The maternal uncle had a major part in decision making in his niece' or nephew's life. Occasions are celebrated with pomp.

The whole house is decorated with fresh flowers. There are flower lei's hanging from the walls and the ceiling. The tables are overflowing with foods and gifts. The aroma of delicious Indian cooking is in the air. There are plenty of men, women and children in the house. They are all dressed in their Sunday best . It seemed like the whole of India had descended to this house. A handful of Europeans mostly neighbors, were there as well. Some of their family from back home have also arrived for the auspicious ceremony. Cheenu was also invited to the occasion. He arrived with a bag load of gifts. Venkat and Priya welcome him and he handed them the gift. Priya went and kept the gift bag on yet another burgeoning table and she rejoined her husband.

Eventually all the invitees have arrived and Venkat gathers them all around his daughter and mother-in-law. "Dear friends and family, Priya and myself welcome you to the naming ceremony of our daughter. Thank you for making the time to come and joining us on this auspicious occasion. Please bless our daughter with all your heart."

Venkat looks at his daughter with deep love and tenderness and speaks to her. "Dear daughter, You are welcome to our family. We consider ourselves the luckiest people ever. Thank you for providing us with the status of parents. We are very blessed to have a child like you in our life. You have filled us with all the happiness that wealth cannot buy and for that we have chosen the name Aishwarya. The name Aishwarya means wealth or prosperity. It goes beyond money. It encompasses happiness of the body, mind and the spirit. So Aishwarya, welcome my darling". All the guests are moved emotionally. Everyone chants her name three times as is the custom. 'Aishwarya----' 'Aishwarya-----' 'Aishwarya------

Aishwarya gives a gurgle in response. Venkat looks at his wife and says fondly to his daughter. "We think that you really like this name." Aishwarya smiles this time and wriggles up and down on her granny's lap. Every one admires her response to her name. Venkat now invites everyone to join at the food table for the buffet. People are now busy serving food for themselves. They acknowledge and wish each other. Venkat introduces people who don't know each other and then let's them get on with the conversation while he moves to another group. Priya and Venkat continue to circulate and network amongst the guest. Priya's mother is sitting on the couch with the baby in her arms. Aishwarya is asleep now oblivious to the celebration which is in full swing. Cheenu extricates himself as he needs to go to the restroom.

Once inside the rest room, Cheenu locks the door. He leans on the door to take a breather. It is good to be away from the crowd. His eyes roam around and take in the objects in the restroom. Suddenly his eyes brighten up with excitement. He sees that there is a golden chain hanging from the mirror. He begins to salivate and hyper ventilate. Obviously it belongs to someone in the family. It looks a bit old fashioned. It might be Priya's mothers. All these thoughts flash in Cheenu's mind. Next minute he is imagining picking up the chain and bringing it to the pawn shop. It will fetch a lot of money. It looks heavy. He can get at least £300 — £400 for it. There are many Indian pawn shops who will be happy to give him that amount. It will be a pittance as far as they are concerned but for Cheenu, in his present state is a huge amount. Imagine using that money for poker. He could win so many jackpots. Cheenu literally salivates at the thought of playing and winning. He quickly picks up the golden chain and pockets it. He has forgotten about using the rest room now. He flushes the toilet and washes his hand. Suddenly he hears someone knocking urgently on the door. Cheenu becomes very tensed.

Priya in a nervous voice, "Hello, who is in there?" Cheenu replies, "Priya, sister its me Cheenu." Priya is relaxed at hearing Cheenu's voice "Thank God, it is you brother. Is there a chain hanging on the mirror? My mum kept it there while getting ready in the evening."

Priya's mother can also be heard now. Priya asks her if she was sure that she had definitely kept the chain in the bathroom. Priya's mother answers in the affirmative. Cheenu's happiness bursts like a balloon. He feels for the chain in his pocket. He is in a dilemma now. He does not want to part with the chain but he can't keep quite either. Not only is it morally wrong but also he will be caught very soon. They may not say anything to him but they will always look at him with suspicion. A tug-O-Yes, war ensues in his head. For a split second, his conscience wins and his rational being takes over. "Yes, sister, I see it here. I will bring it out when I am done."

Priya's voice is filled with relief, "Thanks brother."

Cheenu holds his breath for a few seconds, he heaves a sigh of unaccomplished longing. He pretends to wash his hand and then he walks out from the bathroom with the chain. He smiles at Priya who is waiting outside the bathroom.

She looks at the chain and beams at Cheenu with a satisfied smile, "Thanks brother. I am glad that it is you who went to use the toilet first. It would have been an insult to the other guests if word got out that a chain is lost during a family function. People will look at each other and us with suspicion. Every-time we meet them or we speak to them, they might think that we are speaking in such a manner because we are suspicious. And it is only natural for all of us to think in that way. You are like family so I was able to ask you. I could not have done that with the others. Thank God."

Someone comes into the corridor to use the rest room and smiles at them. Priya smiles back. Once the person has closed the door of the rest room behind them, the three of them walk out quietly.

Cheenu is sitting in a bar with two acquaintances. They are looking tensed. Cheenu is apologetic, "Sorry about this brother but I will repay you next month." Sanjay is irritated now. He pointed out, "Cheenu, you said the same last month."

Cheenu made yet another promise that he was not going to keep. "I will refurnish you with the money on pay day." Sanjay is very agitated and annoyed "Cheenu, you know I need the money for my sister's wedding; which is fixed for next month. They need to pay everyone for the wedding from the caterers to the decorators in advance. You know that in our culture everyone in the family contribute towards the cost of the wedding. I am the elder brother. I am supposed to be the biggest contributor. I am not even answering the phone because I can't come up with the same excuse every time.

Even though it is not true, they will begin to think that I don't want to contribute.

My wife is very unhappy with the situation. Naturally she will be blamed for my reluctance to send the money home. I don't know what to do." Cheenu does not respond. He keeps staring into his glass. Sanjay looks at Cheenu with some disappointment. "Cheenu, you knew my situation when I gave you the money but you are not taking it seriously. Please arrange to give me my money back soon." He throws a few pounds on the table and goes away.

Cheenu is becoming more frustrated everyday. He needs to come up with the money. The situation is strangling him slowly. He thinks of options to deal with it. One day he is walking on the street deep in thought and suddenly he sees Priya's mother walking with the baby in the pram on the other side of the road. He decides to go across to speak to them but suddenly he changes his mind. A dark thought enters his head. In a split second, he comes to the conclusion that he cannot get more borrowings from anyone. People are avoiding him like a plague. The loan shark and his men are paying visits to his house more frequently. What if he kidnapped the baby and asked Venkat for the ransom? Anyone will do that for their child surely! The more he thought about it, the idea strongly took root in his mind. He walked away from there. All day he kept thinking about it. He came up with possible ways of kidnapping. All sorts of questions arose in his mind. Where will he keep the baby? What if he needs to go out? What if the baby needs something and he is not able to understand. Apart from seeing the baby occasionally, he does not know much about it. How will he keep the baby happy? He does not even know how to change a diaper. This does not look like it is going to work.

Wait! What if I kidnap the grandmother as well? Yes, that should work shouldn't it? If I terrify her enough, she will keep her mouth shut. She will also keep the baby quiet. She can change the diaper, she can feed the baby. All he has to do is keep the old lady terrified. With these thoughts in his mind, he goes to sleep. He is more relaxed now. He has a plan to pay of his debt.

Cheenu wakes up a new man. His troubles will be over soon. He is filled with happiness. He steps into the shower and he thinks out his plan in detail. "Where will he hide them?" It won't be long before the police come searching the houses of every Tom, Dick and Harry that Venkat was acquainted to. He will not be able to hide them in his house. A crying baby will draw the neighbors' attention. Is there another place that he can use without getting himself into a fix. There has to be a place.

Cheenu went to work as usual. On the way to work there is a deserted area. Suddenly a thought strikes him. Was there a warehouse on this street? Did he see a homeless man sit outside the building all the time? How was he always sitting there? Surely it has to be empty then. He will check it out this evening on his way back from work.

Cheenu stepped out of the shower and got ready to go to work. With a slight spring in his feet, he walked out of the apartment complex. He took the bus to work today. He could not use private transport. He can't afford to leave a trail after himself. He got on the bus and took the side seat. He was able to see the sights more properly. The River Thames looked very beautiful in the sunlight. A sight he had not noticed for months up until now. Well, what he did not have; he did not miss. Now he will be able to view the city of London in a different light. His troubles will be over soon. He will be a free man. Free of his debts. Free of the loan shark. Free of the shaming looks that his colleagues and friends reserved for him alone. He will be free, free, free. His spirit soared into the sky in a bubble of happiness.

Cheenu worked all day with enthusiasm. He cleared his desk off a lot of work. Even his colleagues noticed the new Cheenu. Venkat remarked at coffee break, "Hey Cheenu, you are smiling. I haven't seen you so happy in a long time. Are you going away on a holiday or what?" Cheenu gushed, "Yes Venkat, I have decided to go home for a while." Venkat is happy for Cheenu, "That's good. When are you going? Is your flight booked?"

Cheenu holds out both of his hands as a signal for Venkat to stop. "Hang on. Not to fast. I am only going to request annual leave today. I hope that the boss is in a good mood. How are Priya and Aishwarya?"

Venkat thinks fondly of his baby, "They are good. I hate to leave the house before Aishwarya wakes up. I love to see her smile. It gets me through the day. Priya is going to work as well now. And she is worse than me. Working mothers are caught between two mountains. One is their baby and the other one is their career . The baby is obviously always first but can't afford for the career to come second. A career will never play second fiddle to a baby."

Cheenu replied with all sincerity, "I know. First babies always do that to the parents. Wait till you have your second and you will be singing a different hymn all together." Venkat is amused at Cheeu's response, "Ha, ha there is a lot of time for that yet. Who knows Aishwarya might be our only child."

Cheenu strikes back with a smile, "Never say never. Well, anyway let me see if the boss is free. So that I can get my annual leave sanctioned." Venkat smiles, "Meet you at lunch then." Cheenu lets him take his leave, "Okay see you."

Venkat goes back to his office with his coffee mug. Cheenu goes near the boss' office in the pretext that he is going to see the boss. Instead he goes to the restroom and comes back to his seat after a while.

That evening Cheenu says goodbye to all his colleagues and walks by the river. He is in his running gear. It is a good way to snoop around. Eventually he reaches the ware house. The homeless guy is no where to be seen. It is peak hours so he has probably gone off to conduct his trade. Everyone has to make a living. Cheenu circled around the warehouse as if he was jogging. No one will become suspicious that way. They will think that he is jogging around the block in circles. It was a very old dirty place. It was deserted. After a few rounds he noted that there was a very tiny crack in the base of the shutter. Ha! That means there is access to the inside. A small one but it didn't really matter. He was very slim. How would he get the old lady in though? She was a reasonably graceful and agile woman but old age does leave its mark on everybody. Well, he will explore the warehouse further first. He will do that tomorrow. He should go home now. He didn't want to rouse any suspicion. Cheenu goes home and sleeps well for two nights in a row. Imagine the sense or relief he had, now that he had a plan.

Cheenu went to work as normal the next day. He worked hard all day. He eventually goes to his boss. Now he is guaranteed annual leave because he has cleared his desk completely. No outstanding projects. Nothing to review and improve. Cheenu mentally pats his shoulder. "Great Cheenu, you can work very satisfactorily when you put your mind to it. You only do that when things are looking up."

In the evening, Cheenu goes jogging again. He just circles the ware house a few times. But he does not approach the place. He has to be very careful. He knows that he does not have the luxury of time but he cannot hurry either. He cannot afford to be caught. He does not see any signs of activity. It is the same as he had seen it for the last two days. Well, he will watch it for a few more days. There are windows on all the floors but most of them are boarded. Some will allow day light to filter through. But they are so dusty on the outside that they will not allow light from the inside to reflect out. He will have to use a small source of light. May be he will use a few candles. It does not look like there is a fire hazard in this place.

Cheenu has got his annual leave sanctioned. He now has to make a few calls to pretend that he is trying to book tickets. Many of his colleagues know a few travel agents. His own company uses a particular travel agent for dignitaries from abroad. He has to go through the motions. He won't be going home for a long time. Everyday Cheenu advanced his plans that much closer to execution. He now has gained entry to the warehouse. He has widened the opening of the shutter and boarded it back. Now he knew that he could bring the grandmother through the small opening.

Strangers Inside

He has not roused anyone's curiosity yet which is good.

He chooses a room which is in the middle floor, right in the centre. You have to go through a few more rooms to be able to look out the window on either side of the building. That is good. Light from the candle won't creep out. The middle portion will release heat slower than the exterior at night. That means he does not have to keep an extra source of heat. Large candles will keep the three of them warm. It will be only two days. He has to give Venkat the opportunity to gather the money together. It is a large sum after all.

Cheenu slowly begins to furnish the middle room of the warehouse with the basic needs. He has checked it thoroughly. It even has an ensuite toilet. That's excellent! Cheenu rubs his hands in glee. He doesn't have to clean a commode. Cheenu goes home that evening and gets his dumbbells out. He exercises for a while to get the adrenaline going. He then purposefully drops the dumbbell on to his feet. He clenches his teeth together to stop him from crying. He then goes to the GP's office in a taxi. He hobbles in. He is in a lot of pain now. The idea does not seem appealing anymore but it had to be done. The GP orders an x-ray and diagnoses a broken toe. He straps the toes together except for the big toe to provide support for the broken one. The GP provides him with a certificate of absence from work. Next day Cheenu rings his office to inform of his unexpected accident and posts his certificate of illness to the office.

Everything is set to go now. He just needs to decide how he can deliver the ransom note without detection. How to get the old lady and the baby to come with him quietly. He will need to work the brain cells harder. It is not going to be easy. The old lady looks like a shrewd woman.

Well, first things first. What is the best way to deliver the letter? Will it be a messenger? No what a foolish thought. The courier? No, it's traceable. The post box to their house? No, there is a camera in the vicinity. What should it be? What will it be? What will it be? Ha! It has to be the postman because then Cheenu will not be anywhere near their house on the day. That's it! It's the postman's job to deliver the letter, isn't ? That's what it will be. Okay so that is sorted. What next? Yes, the lady and the baby! That should not be difficult. He has to prevent her from becoming suspicious. Enough work for the brain cells today. The hands have begun to shiver now. "I need a game of poker right now."

Cheenu goes off to the pub. He plays a few sets with no luck, then he returns home. He sleeps better now. Next day he gets up later than usual. He had a leisurely breakfast and then he gets ready to go out. He did not have to go anywhere in a hurry. It was around this time he had seen the old lady going for a walk with the baby. So it should be all right to snoop around their house for a while. He went jogging in his sports wear and after a few rounds around the block, he sat down on a bench near Venkat's house for a very slow drink from his bottle. He saw the postman coming on his bicycle. One house at a time, he stopped to drop a few letters. He skipped one or two houses and then he did the same thing again. Off his bike and into the front garden, up-to the front door, dropped the letter into the post box and then back again on his bike. Repeat again at the next set of houses. Cheenu averted his eyes away from him. He has to stop gawking or someone might notice. Here comes the buggy with the baby inside it and the lady pushing from behind. He has to move cautiously. She should not recognise him. She will say it to Venkat and Priya.

There are only two things Venkat talks about in the office. His baby and the grandmother. How she cooks and how she tells them the events of the day. Of course she will. She is lonely here. And that is something he needs to confirm before attempting the kidnapping. He has to make sure that she has not made any acquaintances on her daily walks. A beautiful baby will draw any one to a chat.

His leg is hurting. He shouldn't have been too enthusiastic about his jog. Well, he will pop a few pain killers when he gets home. Time to move on. At least the self inflicted harm wasn't that bad. Cheenu hobbles home slowly. He takes a few pain killers, adds some milk to the cereal packet and eats it. He misses home cooked food. He misses his mother's cooking. He will go home, soon. Once his debts are all sorted! He goes to the toilet, comes out and gets into bed to sleep.

Next day Cheenu went out to the bus stop near Venkat's house. It was raining. He had his hood on and an umbrella. He was quiet sure that he wouldn't see the old lady today. He waited for a while and the lady did not come. He did see the postman though. So that is going to occur regardless of the weather. He has to follow the lady for one more day and then he can execute his plan. He now knows that he cannot pick a rainy day. It just won't work. Also it will leave trails around the empty; now not so empty warehouse.

Okay tomorrow is predicted to be a dry day. Hope the weatherman or weather woman is correct. In his country it was accurate prediction because the opposite of the weather-forecast will always happen. So if it was predicted to be rainy then you don't have to bring the umbrella with you ha, ha. Cheenu sits down at the table with a cup of coffee by his elbow. He begins to formulate the contents of the ransom note. What should he write? How should the note begin? Well, start writing and it will follow through. Okay here goes......

VENKY, YOUR DAUGHTER AND MOTHER-IN-LAW ARE SAFE FOR NOW. IF YOU WANT THEM BACK

ALIVE AND WELL THEN, BRING EIGHTY-THOUSAND POUNDS TO BARBARA KENDALL'S GRAVE AT THE KENSAL GREEN CEMETERY AT 6 PM THIS EVENING. DON'T TRY TO ACT SMART OR GO TO THE POLICE, IF YOU WANT TO SEE THEM IN ONE PIECE.

He hides the letter under his mattress. He goes to check the warehouse to see that it is not disturbed. It isn't. Neither the owner or the homeless man has come back. Moreover he has barred the entrance and it is holding firmly. "Good job One more day... all my troubles will be over"

Next day Cheenu went out to the bus stop again. Yes, the old lady is there. The weather-forecast was accurate. Today is a dry day just as predicted. I am sure the baby did not give the old lady an easy time yesterday for staying indoors. No wonder she is early today. "Good! Tomorrow is the big day."

Cheenu goes back home. He then went out to the supermarket and added more things to his ever growing list. Duct tape, rope to tie the old lady, food and bottled water, nappies and oh yes baby milk. Get small packs of all the brand that are available. Don't know what the child will prefer. "Why does a small baby need so much?" Well, you can't keep a crying baby quiet. An adult can be threatened to keep quite or even clunked on the head, but a baby will have less comprehension and cry louder. Oh and some tinned food. The old lady will have to go without the tasty meals that she cooks.

THE ABDUCTION

The morning breaks out bright and cheerful. There is a slight cool breeze which is very refreshing. The pollution so unique to London has been washed out by the heavy rain of two days ago. Cheenu looks forward to the time enthusiastically. If the postman delivers the letter successfully then, today is the day for the kidnap.

He begins to follow the postman. The postman goes into an estate and Cheenu bypasses the estate and walks ahead. He goes to the corner deli shop and buys a pack of cigarettes. He waits for the postman while he smokes. The postman is coming out. Good he has to get ready now. He follows the postman at a distance. He has the envelope containing the letter in his hands now. At one place, the street turns a corner. A person can be hidden there by the bushes which has overgrown its boundaries of one of the front yards. Here he will be near the postman and yet he won't be visible for a while. Good that is the correct spot to execute his plan. The postman goes past the bend. Cheenu drops the letter at the bend and walks away for a few steps. Then he does an about turn and starts walking towards the postman. "Oh no, a lady is walking towards me." She looks at the envelope on the ground and looks back at the postman. She calls out to the postman and hands him the letter. The postman thanks her and hurriedly walks away. Poor young lad, he is embarrassed by his perceived mistake. He pushes the envelope back into the bundle. That was excellent. He didn't even have to do the job as he had planned. The lady did it for him as if she could read his thoughts. Fantastic! Cheenu rubbed his hands in glee. He followed the postman discreetly up to Venkat's house. Yes,! He has gone into the gate. He can see him push the envelope in through the post box in the front door. Fantastic! Now to go and find the old lady. He behaved like the fox in the tale of Red Riding Hood. Ready to trick the old woman. 'Grandma........., here I come for you-'. He walked away to the usual route that the old lady took everyday. He had been watching her for so many days. The route is etched into his memory. It is a person's predictability and sticking to habit which makes him vulnerable. But if a person is not habitual then it means that the person is living with the fear of something bad happening around the corner. A calm person will go about his job in the same manner everyday which makes him predictable and an easy target.

Back to the present in the interrogation room..........

Cheenu requests a bathroom break. A deputy brings him out to the toilet. Brenda takes a sip of water from her water glass. John sits and looks at the notes that he had made so far. Dev has his hands knotted behind his head and stares up at the ceiling. No one is speaking. They are waiting for the events to unfold. What they have heard so far does not come anywhere near the gruesomeness they saw in the warehouse.

The clock kept doing its job. A few minutes later, Cheenu walked into the room with the deputy. He sits down on the chair. He takes a sip of water from his glass. Brenda refills it again.

Dev turns on the tape-recorder as before. He speaks into the tape-recorder-the time, the date, the personnel and the nature of the interrogation. "Cheenu, you wrote the ransom note by your hand?" Cheenu replied that he had. Dev queried, "Were you not worried that you will be caught?" Cheenu replied cockily, "No I was very sure that Venkat will not go to the police. He will want his daughter back so he will bring the money. The old lady will only tell Venkat who was responsible when she was returned safely to her family with the baby. I knew that he will keep it quiet because he got his baby back. He will not trust me after that. But I had decided to go home after

my debts are finished, never to return."
Dev was astonished, "If you were so
confident, then why did you change your
handwriting? You are right handed aren't
you? Cheenu confirmed that he was.

Dev passes a piece of blank paper to
Cheenu, "Can you write the same note
with your left hand." Cheenu looks at
John and John nods in agreement. "I
can't remember what I wrote," he said.
Dev replied, "You do not have to
duplicate the whole ransom note as it is.
Write what ever you remember from it."

Cheenu wrote with his left hand on the
piece of paper. "VENKY, YOUR
DAUGHTER AND MOTHER-IN-
LAW ARE SAFE WITH ME. BRING
EIGHTY-THOUSAND POUNDS
FOR THEIR RELEASE.

Dev asked him, "Can you sign that to
agree that you wrote it without any
pressure or coercion. We already know
that you wrote the original ransom note

with your left hand. What we don't understand is if you were not afraid to use your own handwriting then why did you use your left hand?"Cheenu replied, "Just on the off chance that Venkat did go to the police." Dev asked, "So you were kind of expecting that it might happen?" Cheenu replied, "No I was not. But it was a just in case thing."

Dev moved over to the next question, "Did you possess any kind of weapon?" Cheenu said that he had a revolver. Dev asked him if it was the same revolver that he tried to use at the casino? And Cheenu answered, "Yes". Dev clarified, "Did you have any intention of using the revolver on them?"

Cheenu hastily said, "No, I was going to send them back safely." Dev wanted to know if Cheenu was under the influence of alcohol or drugs? Cheenu said, "Not at the time when I kidnapped them, but later yes"

Dev wanted to confirm if it was one or both. "Which, alcohol or drug?" Cheenu confirmed that it was both. Dev asked, "When did you use those?" Cheenu said that once he had realised that Venkat had called the police; he was very upset. Dev and Brenda looked at each other. "When did you realise that?" Cheenu said that he gathered that when he saw the police arrive at the Kensal Green Cemetery posing as a funeral procession.

Dev commented, "You were hiding in the branches of the tree in the seating area" Cheenu replied, "Yes, I was waiting for Venkat so I was watching with my binoculars for his arrival. The tree was the best and nearest cover. Dev wanted to know further, "What made you think that they were the police?"

Cheenu said that their handguns were sticking out from under the coats. You could make out the shape from under their jackets. That made it certain." Dev asked, "And?" Cheenu replied, "Venkat confirmed it by not looking at the procession at all. He just left the bag as I had asked him to. Were they not the police; he would have waited until the funeral party had left to keep the bag. But he neither looked up nor waited. He just kept the bag, turned around and left. That confirmed my suspicion.

Dev asked, "Why did you particularly choose Venkat and his wife for the ransom? There are so many other rich people you could have been targeted."

Cheenu said that he knew them, "I knew them and their habits. They were both working in good jobs so I figured that they had the money. Priya always had gold on her. She changed her jewels quite frequently. The old lady also had a heavy enough gold chain around her neck. The baby was also decked in gold all the time. I knew that the old lady will have brought some jewels from India when she came over for the birth of the baby. They spoke the same language as me. That meant that I could lure the grandmother to come with me without creating any problem.

Dev asked, "How long were you planning this for?" "Five or six days" Cheenu countered. Dev wanted to know more about him, "Did you have a change of mind at any time during these five to six days?" Cheenu spread his hands out, "No I was desperate. All I could think of was that I need the money." Dev is frustrated now, "If you were so desperate, why did you not take the money?"

Cheenu smartly replied, "I was definite now that the police were involved so I thought that the currency will be marked as well. Or there may be a tracker in the bag." Dev looked at him: So going back to where you had stopped. How did you get the grandmother to come with you without causing any commotion?"

Cheenu continued with the story

Here comes the old lady with the buggy. The baby has its favourite teddy towel wrapped around her finger. He had seen it fall one day and after a while the woman had come back with a screaming baby to look for the towel. He has to be careful with that towel. He walks casually across to the old lady. "Hello mother, how are you?"

She was surprised to see Cheenu, "Oh hello Cheenu! What are you doing here? I heard that you were on sick leave." Cheenu replied, "Yes mother, I was doing my daily exercise and the dumbbell fell on my feet." Mother with genuine concern in her voice, "You should be more careful. Is it any better now? I can prepare you an herbal remedy for it. The remedy is made of turmeric and tamarind. Come back to the house with me and I will prepare that for you."

Cheenu thanked the lady, "Sure mother. Were you going somewhere?" She looked at the baby indulgently, "Yes I go for a stroll with the baby everyday. But if your leg is painful, we can go back now." Cheenu is temporarily overwhelmed by the old lady's concern. Desperately he says, "Oh no mother! It's not that bad. The doctor said that I need the exercise. We can finish the walk and then go home". Cheenu further adds: "Let me push the buggy for you". Mother said disbelievingly, "No Cheenu, your leg is hurt."

Cheenu is frustrated now, "No mother, that is why I need the buggy. I had thought that I was feeling better so I did not bring the walking stick. But now I think that I need to lean on something. It's not as if I am going to lift it."

Mother is reassured now and grudgingly replied, "Okay then." Both of them walk silently for a while. Cheenu notices that there is a phone inside the buggy near the baby. He has to get that. He continues to walk quietly. The baby gurgles at Cheenu and Cheenu smiles back and responds to her. She is so beautiful.... She will melt anyone's heart. Suddenly the baby drops its toy on the road.

Cheenu disregards it and keeps walking. The grandmother bends down to pick up the toy. Cheenu uses this opportunity to pick up the phone from the buggy and quickly pockets it. It was perfect timing because just then the phone vibrates. He will have to switch it off very soon. He gets the toy from the grandmother and gives it back to the baby. "Mother did you do any sightseeing, since you arrived to the UK?"

Mother said, "Yes, Venkat brought us out to the Giant wheel, the beach and the flower market. He said that there is a rose garden nearby. We will go there next weekend and to see the palace." Cheenu exclaimed, "That's excellent. Venkat has brought you to some of the tourist places. And you do have more time to see the other attractions. There is an exhibition five minutes from here. Shall we go there today?" The old lady looks at him in some confusion and indecision. "Cheenu I have to cook for Aishwarya."

Cheenu reassured her, "It's okay mother. It is only going to take half an hour. You have plenty of time. I can call Venkat now and tell him that you are with me and that we will be late." He takes out his mobile and pretends to call Venkat. "Venkat, how are you? ------- I am good, feeling much better. I am with Aishwarya and mother. I was thinking if it will be all right to bring them to the exhibition. -------- Okay that's great. Shall I hand over the phone to mother......?" Then he acts as if Venkat is on the other end of the phone and he asks Venkat to hold on for one moment. He then hands over the phone to the old lady.

Mother smilingly takes the phone from Cheenu: "Hello Venkat, Hello----" She looks puzzlingly at Cheenu. "He is not saying anything" Cheenu acts puzzled and takes the phone back from the old lady and listens carefully. Then he looks at the screen. "Mother the phone is disconnected somehow. He had said that he was busy."

Mother disappointedly smiles "Priya always tells me that he thinks that I talk a lot. If he is busy then he probably got terrified that I will talk to him for long. Wise guy, I get so lonely here Cheenu! You know back home, I am surrounded by the people I know. Many people come and go. The extended families visit for one reason or the other. Even the street vendors will speak to you while you are selecting and choosing their ware. The girls in the supermarket here don't even look at you. Them chewing their bubblegums all the time! It's not the same here and I also don't know the language. Aishwarya keeps me busy. If not for her, I would have caught the first flight home."

Cheenu agrees, "Yes mother. Life is very lonely here. That's because we don't have our families with us. We can't call in on anyone casually. Everything needs to be pre-organized. There is no fun in it. I know that there is no other way around it. People are so busy here. Everyone has to lead their own life and they do so behind closed doors. Partly because of the weather and partly because of the perception of privacy." They keep walking for a good while.

Mother looks around the area, "Cheenu where are we going? Why is this place so dirty?" Cheenu replies, "Mother we are taking a short cut. My leg is hurting. Can we sit down for a few minutes?" The old lady frowned, "Cheenu, there is no place here to sit down." Cheenu points to the distance,   "Mother, see that building there? If we go into that building, we will be out from the cold. It is the cold that causes more pain."

Mother is not happy. "That place looks empty. Will someone not be angry?" Cheenu laughed, "No mother, I know the guy who owns the building. He works with me. He will not mind."

Mother complies, "Okay if you think it is wise to do so". They reach the building. Cheenu brings them in. They sit there for a while. Cheenu unties his shoe laces and gives his toes a good wriggle. He shows his toe to the lady. It is purple-black all around the strapped area. The lady looks at him in sympathy and promises to prepare the remedy as soon as they get home. When she thinks that Cheenu has had enough rest. She asks him "Cheenu, shall we go? I would like to use a rest room. Aishwarya will soon need her nappy changed."

Cheenu smiles. "That is no problem. There is a rest room inside this building. Let's use that. We can roll the buggy to the service lift and then reach the place." They keep ascending the building via the lift. Mother looks around, "This place is so lonely. It is terrifying." Cheenu reassures her, "It's okay mother. I am here with you." They get out of the lift when it stops. Cheenu brings them to the room.

Mother is surprised. "Cheenu, this place is so clean. It doesn't even look like a part of this building." The old lady looks around in curiosity. Cheenu uses this opportunity to his advantage. He reaches behind the old lady and clamps her mouth with a cloth. Cheenu ties her two hands at the back together with a rope. He then turns the lady around who is so shocked that she complies. Her eyes are wide in horror. He looks her in the eye and says: 'I am sorry mother but I need the money so I have kidnapped you and the baby. I will not hurt you. I will return you safe to Venkat and Priya; once I get the money."

Cheenu continues, "I am going to remove the cloth from your mouth. Please don't scream. No one is going to hear you." He then sits her on the floor and removes the cloth from her mouth.

The lady looks at Cheenu and pleads: Please Cheenu, don't do this. I don't know what is wrong but I can understand that you need money. I have some money with me. Come home with me, I will give it to you. I will ask Priya to help you. Venkat will agree to whatever Priya says. We won't tell him about this. Priya will get the money to get you out of what ever trouble you are in. Please let us go. Please take us back home to our family."

Cheenu sits at the table and thinks for a while: 'No mother, the money you have will not be enough for me. Venkat will need to know why you need such a big amount. I have kept food for you both. Please co-operate and once I get the money, I will let you go. This will all end well by this evening. The old lady screams, "Cheenu plea-----se listen."

Cheenu is very irritated now. "Mother, stop pleading now. I have to go out somewhere. I will be back soon." He then unties the rope, brings her arms to the front and reties it. This gives her some movement in her arms. Blood begins to flow back into her wrist. She will try and loosen the knot when he goes.

Cheenu warns, "Mother, I am going now. Please don't do anything stupid. You will not be able to get out of here however much you try. I will not be happy to see that you did not pay attention to what I said." Cheenu goes out of the room. He locks the door behind him. She listens intently. She does not hear anything.

Tears run down the old woman's cheeks. She is now alternating between anger at him for kidnapping them and anger at herself for being so gullible. But why would she suspect him? She had treated him like a son. That is the custom and the culture in their country. He should have given her the respect she deserved. Instead he has kidnapped her and Aishwarya. Oh the poor baby. She is so young and tender. He has promised not to hurt but a man who stooped to kidnap both of them will not stop at anything to get the money. Hope Venkat comes up with the money soon. Not for her but for the baby She has lived her life and will have no regrets about dying. The only regret will be that she broke her daughter's trust. Her daughter trusted me-her mother with her daughter and I failed to keep her safe. What kind of a mother that makes her?

As a mother, she is supposed to keep her children happy. But her daughter will go through pain today. Worse than the pain of labour, the labour pain was worth something beautiful in the end. The way she looked at her daughter in wonder and awe was so touching. The midwives had given the baby straight to her and how she had hugged her so tightly. Even the midwives were moved. They covered them both with blankets and kept them warm. They called this skin-to-skin care and said that the baby will begin breastfeeding soon. And as if Aishwarya was waiting to perform! She began moving to the breast and took the breast into her mouth. It was an act of ownership and yet she was so gentle to her mother. Priya did not feel any pain or discomfort. There was such a calmness in that moment. The golden moment etched for ever in their memories.

Venkat was in tears, so moved with tenderness for his wife. You could see him transform into a father in that very minute. Fiercely protective and yet so vulnerable, He could understand the weight of his responsibility in that minute and you could see the determination in his face. And now-----? And now all his courage and love is being challenged. Do they know yet? Has this horrible man told them yet? Poor Priya! How is she coping? She will be so distraught with grief. She did not even like to go to work leaving her baby with her own mother. She didn't like to separate from Aishwarya even for one minute. Poor Priya, now she will be in agony. How I wish I could turn the clock just one hour back? And be in the safety of our house.

Cheenu would not have been able to kidnap them from there.

All these thoughts ran through her mind but she did not react except for the large drops of tears dripping over the buggy. In that split second when he was stuffing her mouth with the cloth, she had seen a madness in his eyes. It was a very dangerous kind of lunacy. She has to be careful with him and keep him calm or he will harm them. At least Aishwarya is asleep-for now. What will happen when she wakes up and cries?

"Oh my God!" What is she doing sitting and reminiscing? She has to get the baby out of here. She looks at the rope. She brings it to her mouth. And begins to try undoing the rope. 'It is very tight. It is not moving, Ok calm down, relax, take a deep breath. Try again." Oh why is this so tight. He really meant it. "I cannot undo the rope. I will try the door". She tries to bite the rope to soften it and make it loose. It tasted horrible but she tried to loosen it as much as she can but to no avail.

Next she tried the door with her hand, no movement. She tried pushing the door with her hips, nope! Then she heaved her whole body against the door and pushed for a long time. Her face became very red with exertion. She is becoming very frustrated now. Next she tried the wall. She tapped on it with her bound hands. She heard a lot of fluttering. She held her breath to concentrate. No more sound, she banged the walls again. "He-----lp" and yet more fluttering, They sound like birds. She did see pigeons fly around low in the sky when she was coming in to the building with him. "OH--I curse that moment." She doesn't give up but with every cry for help, her voice becomes heavier with desperation. Her face becomes redder and redder with each exertion. Her breath becomes shallower and shallower. Yet she does not give up. She is a strong woman but even strong people have their limits. She did not have the strength to defy this particular odd.

ALL HELL BREAKS LOOSE

Meanwhile, Priya rang her husband Venkat on his mobile to check if he was on the phone speaking to her mother. No, she can hear it dialling. Venkat picked up at the second ring. "Hello Priya?" Priya answered, "Venkat: Did you speak to mother. She is not answering her phone." Venkat replied, "Priya, I rang her as usual when she would have been on her walk with Aishwarya. But she did not answer. So I thought that she was busy with her. I expected her to call back by now. This is very unusual. Did you call her?"

Priya said, "Yes I did. But she is not answering. The phone seems to be dead now." Venkat suggests, "Priya, do one thing. Take permission from your boss and go home. She should be back from her walk now. She is an old woman after all. She may have become tired and may have fallen asleep with the baby."

Priya thinks that it is a good plan. She will get to see her baby in the middle of the day. What a pleasant surprise! "Okay, I will do that." Venkat calms her down, "Don't hurry. Take your time and be safe. I will keep ringing her and if she answers me. I will ask her to call you straightaway. Is that okay?" Priya said, "Yes that is a good plan. I will leave now." Venkat bade goodbye to her. Priya disconnected the phone, "Bye".

Venkat looked at the display of the mobile. Then he takes a deep breath and rings his mother-in-law again. But there is no answer. The phone is dead. May be she has plugged it into the socket to charge the battery and forgot to turn it on. He will try and finish his work and then take permission after lunch. He wants to see his daughter as well. He has been missing her smile since this morning. She was asleep when he left for work.

Priya drives the car through the shortest route possible. She reaches home in record time and finds the house locked. She calls out to her mother. 'Mom, I am home. Aishu darling, I am home.' Meanwhile she unlocks the door with her own key. Usually her mother will hear the key on the door and will come and stand out in the corridor with the baby. She knows that Priya and Aishwarya both love that. They reach for each other straight away and rain kisses on each other. Aishwarya is full of words, excitement and cheer as soon as she sees her mother. She is a happy child. But today her mother is not standing in the door way with her baby. "Where is she?" Priya goes straight to the kitchen. Her mother has left it sparkling clean as usual. Lunch is not ready which is usually cooked by this time. Aishwarya eats softly cooked rice and dal at one o' clock. Her mother is never late where Aishwarya is concerned. That meant that they all got fed on time. Venkat always remarks on the regularity of the meals since mom arrived. Poor man, he had to wait for her to finish cooking. She took ages to cook and not as half as tasty as what her mother made. Priya smiles at the thought. She walks over to Aishwarya's bedroom. Her mom will be in there. "Mom! Are you in there?" She opens the door to the bedroom which is dark and quiet. No one in there, she turns on the light. The buggy was not there in the corridor. Aishwarya's scarf is missing. So they are not back from their walk. "Are they all right? Are they hurt? Did something happen?" A sense of panic now envelops Priya. She rings Venkat on his mobile again. Venkat answers at the first ring. "Priya?"

Priya is anxious. "Venkat they are not back from their walk. I am worried now. I will drive around the usual route that she takes." Venkat hastily dissuades her, "No Priya, wait. Stay at home. She may have gone to the shops. May be she decided to cook something nice for us as a surprise. I have taken permission from my manager. I will drive home along the usual route that they take for their walk. You stay in the house just in case they arrive by the time I get there. At least one of us will know that they are fine."

Priya replies in a tearful voice. "Okay Venkat, please come fast." Venkat reassures her, "I will be there soon baby. I promise you they are fine. I will bring them back with me. Okay?" Priya is pacified, "Okay." He can hear the smile in her voice now. "Thank God". He could never bear to see Priya cry. Even when they had small disagreements, he would be the one to make the peace. He loved his wife so much.

Venkat hangs up the phone. Everyone in the office   is reassuring him that everything will be fine.   They were so attached to the old woman and her granddaughter. Venkat loved them so much. Always speaking about them; The old woman was a 'lady' and always full of hospitality. There was anxiety in all their faces.

Priya goes to the toilet. She comes out from there. She is definite that her mother has not come back from her walk. She usually hangs the clothes out to dry after she comes back. She opens the back door. There are no clothes drying in the back yard. She closes the back door and turns around to go to the master bedroom-their bedroom. Her mother never goes in there. But she will check-just in case. May be Aishwarya threw one of her tantrums and her mother brought her in there to distract her. They may have fallen asleep on the rocking chair which Priya uses for breastfeeding. She can see the inside of the front door from where she is standing. There is an envelope on the floor. Was it there when she arrived? She does not remember seeing it. But then she does not remember keeping her bag on the corner table either! She was so focussed on looking for her mother and daughter. She walks to the front door. She looks down at the envelope. It may have fallen from the post box when the door closed automatically. She bends to look at it.

Something is off. But she can't comprehend what it is.

She picks up the letter. It does not have a stamp. "That's what it is." Does it mean that it was hand delivered? She opens the door to see if someone is in the vicinity who might have hand delivered it. She walks out into the front path with the envelope in her hand. She slits open the envelope. She looks at the words swimming in front of her. She rings her husband urgently. Venkat answers at the first ring. "Priya, I am looking for them." Priya with a wail, "Venka---t come straight home.......No please come now." Venkat is perplexed, "Priya, what's wrong?" Only crying with a pain of pure agony can be heard.

Venkat knows he will not understand even one word now. He sighs, "I am coming. Speak to me baby. Don't disconnect the phone. Speak to me." He hears a thud and then the phone goes dead. He looks at the phone, it is disconnected. He drops it to the floor and then he accelerates his car. Priya was on the mobile speaking to Venkat when a police car went cruising by. The policeman remarked to his companion.

Male Police Constable "What's wrong with that lady? She looks very off color. Oh no please stop the car. She has collapsed." Female Policewoman stops the car and said to him"Okay, I will park the car on the curb and join you." The policeman runs out of the car, the minute it halts. The policewoman Imelda, parks the car at the curb and walks down to Priya's house. She has her walkie talkie. She speaks into the walkie talkie. "Alpha Romeo 1 reporting to base. A woman has collapsed. Possibly at her own front door. Mathew has gone to check. I am joining him now." Meanwhile Mathew calls out to Priya: "Hey lady! Are you okay?" No response from her, he sits on his knees beside her and shakes her gently. Again no response, he picks up her hand and checks her pulse. The pulse is strong and steady. Imelda joins him now and they look at each other. Imelda speaks into her walkie talkie: "Alpha Romeo 1 to base. Need an ambulance asap. A young woman has collapsed outside her front door. Steady pulse and regular respiration."

They turn Priya to her left lateral position with her chin tucked into her chest. Mathew nudges Imelda on the shoulder and points to the envelope. Imelda says, "I will check that letter out. It might not be even in English. Can you go into the house and get a blanket? Need to keep her warm. We can't move her just in case something is broken.

Imelda tries to gently pull the letter out of Priya's fist with her gloved hands. She looks at the content of the letter and she is in shock. It has been written in the English language. She speaks into the walkie-talkie. Simultaneously she pats Priya's body all the way from the top to the bottom. "Alpha Romeo 1 reporting to base. Looks like a case of kidnapping.

The lady was holding a ransom note in her hand. Need more support. She is unconscious now. We are moving the lady into the house. She collapsed when she read the letter. Don't feel the presence of any fractures." Just then Mathew comes out of the house with a blanket. Imelda looks at Mathew and hands him the letter."We need to move her in. Let me try and wake her first. See if she will respond."

Imelda taps Priya on her shoulder. "Hello lady get up. Hello". She taps Priya sharply on the shoulders. Priya comes around and looks at them blankly. She looks at the policewoman in confusion.

Imelda speaks to her kindly, "Hello there, welcome back. We were on our usual patrol and we saw you collapse to the floor." Priya suddenly remembers everything. She begins to cry. 'My sweet daughter, Oh my God! I don't know who took her and my poor mother" Imelda reasons with her, "Calm down. Let's go inside the house."

The two police officers support her to walk into the house. They seat her on the couch and give her a glass of water. She waves the water away. She is very upset and trembling with fear. She looks at them, "Please go away. Please he said no police. Please go away."

Imelda remarks: "Hey lady, my name is Imelda. Please calm down for a few minutes. We need to at least write a report. What is your name?" Priya whose eyes are wide like a saucer, "My name is Priya. I have a two year old daughter. My mother took her for a walk and they have not returned. I saw this note on the floor. I don't know what to do." Imelda asks her kindly, "Is there anyone you can contact?" Priya replies, "My husband is on his way."

Imelda and Mathew look at each other. Suddenly there is a sound of police sirens. Two more patrol cars drive up to the house. They are inside the house now. The police are all over the place. Priya is still sitting on the couch and crying. Imelda gives her a few hand towels to use. Venkat parks in his regular slot and looks at his house in confusion. He tries to walk in to the house. Two of the police constables are posted at the gate. They stop Venkat and make enquiries. Venkat informs them that he lives in the house. Mathew sees this exchange and comes over to the gate. He takes Venkat's hand in his hand and introduces himself. 'My name is Mathew. Imelda and myself saw your wife collapse on the floor. We know from the ransom note that your baby has been kidnapped." The color drains from Venkat's face. He looks at Priya and walks over to her. Priya sees him then and reaches out for him with a wail. Venkat asks angrily. Only the word 'kidnapped registers in his brain. "What is happening here? Where is your mother?"

Priya wails, "Venkat! She has been kidnapped as well." Venkat is dumb struck. To him it seems if he has been punched. All the breath from his lungs gets sucked out. Venkat keeps his hand on his head and another hand on his waste. "Oh my God! What are we going to do? How do you know? Is there a ransom note? What does it say?"

Imelda moves over to Venkat. She hands him the letter and sympathises with him. She explains how they happened to be at the scene. Venkat reads the note and looks up at them accusingly "But he says no police in the note. Why are you here? Please go away. He will harm my child and my mother-in-law."

Imelda understands his panic, "Venkat please calm down. You did not call us here. We witnessed your wife collapsing. We could not just leave her lying like that. If you don't want us to pursue this any further then, say it to us and we will go away."

Venkat is in an absolute dilemma. He looks at his wife in despair. He can see that she is also very confused but she is a mother and she is probably thinking that the police should help them to bring their baby back. He cannot deny Priya help from the police. She will never forgive him if anything happened especially when the police have offered to help in any way.

He calms down and apologises for being rude. "Okay, sorry. I----I did not mean to doubt your capabilities. I just don't know what to do. I just want my baby and my mother-in-law back." Imelda reassures him. "Please don't worry Venkat. We will do all we can." Very soon, Venkat's home begins to look like a miniature police headquarter.

The Kensal Green cemetery is surrounded by trees on all four sides. It is a place of tranquility for those who rest there and for those who come to visit. In the far corner there is a group of trees which provide privacy to those who want to mourn quietly. Cheenu is settled over the branches of one of the trees in that group. He has a binocular in his hand. He scans the entire perimeter of the cemetery through his binoculars. His binocular crosses the gate and suddenly he sweeps back to the gate. A procession of black cars is arriving to the gate. "This is not good". He did not anticipate this. "Now Venkat will have to wait. I hope that they finish burying who ever they brought and go soon."

All the cars come to a halt in the parking lot. Just the black limousine moves a little bit more forward to facilitate the removal of the funeral box. There are many people embarking from the cars. The funeral directors have blue tooth on their ears. Cheenu watches them all very carefully. Some of the people are moving to the edge of the trees. "That is strange. Why are they going there?" Something is really fishy here. He looks at the faces again. They do look like funeral directors in their black coats and white shirts. But something is definitely out of place. Something about their walk and what is that is sticking out? "Ah so that's what it is." He can see a gun sticking out from someone's waist like a beacon. If he did not have the binoculars, he would have been caught. "So Venkat did not pay heed to what he had said in the ransom note. He had said "No police" and yet Venkat went to the police. Now he will pay the price for that. How dare he defy me and go to the police? How dare he? Here"s his car coming in the driveway" Venkat parked the car and got out. He has a briefcase in his hand. He is looking at each grave that he is passing by. He has now seen Barbara Kendall's grave and is walking towards it. He is not paying attention to the people around him. No one is paying him any attention either. "People are supposed to be curious! This behaviour is against the very grain of human nature." There is another one in the near corner; whose gun is sticking out. Also there is non-verbal communication going on there. "Well, Venkat, this is it! You have gone to the police against my advice." Venkat keeps the suitcase beside Barbara's grave and he looks around the cemetery. He studiously avoids the funeral procession. He then walks away from there back into the parking lot and drives away in his car.

Cheenu is very annoyed at Venkat now. He has witnessed everything that has happened. He does not need to know any further. He waits for a good while. The police cannot keep up the pretext of burying someone forever. They will be waiting in vain. The policemen wait for a long time. They have already checked the perimeter. They reluctantly leave after a while. Once they have gone, Cheenu jumps down from the tree. He aims to go to the warehouse straightaway. As he walks on the street, he recognises a drug peddler. He goes up to him and after a few minutes conversation, he buys drugs from him. He goes to the warehouse. The old lady is sitting on the sofa. She has been crying for a long time. She continues to sniffle. The baby is asleep on the sofa.

Cheenu can hear the old woman crying and begging but he does not look at her. He is very angry. He goes into the toilet and sits quietly for a while after his ablution. He uses a needle to inject the drug into himself and keeps the syringe on top of the cistern. He is so agitated that the syringe actually slips further unintentionally and falls into the gap between the cistern and the wall. He becomes more and more angry as the injection takes effect. His decision to kill the old woman and the baby entrenches firmly in his mind.

He comes out of the toilet and looks at the old woman. Her hands are bruised and bleeding from her attempts to escape. The sight of blood fills him with an unexplained exhilaration. The old lady again urges him to let them go. But Cheenu does not have any intention to let them go. He has only one goal. Pay back!

He sits on a stool across from the woman and looks at her. "Mother! Venkat did not pay attention to what I said. I told him not to go to the police. But he did not listen. He made a big mistake". The drug completely has taken over Cheenu's brain by now. He is not in a position to listen to anyone. Suddenly the baby wakes up and begins to cry. Cheenu gets irritated. The old lady looks at the baby helplessly. Her hands are tied but she was able to feed the baby the milk from the sipper that she had brought with her and the baby had gone back to sleep after a while. She begins to reach over to the baby. Her eyes are pleading with Cheenu to reconsider his decision. But Cheenu is in another world altogether. A world that is complicated by drugs, tension, money trouble, gambling addiction and lack of remorse catalysed by the drug.

The baby's cry adds to Cheenu's irritation. The lady's mumbling causes a jarring sound in his ears. Cheenu begins to shout and scream. The baby cries louder on seeing a very acquainted person angry, which infuriates him further. He suddenly keeps his hand on the baby's mouth to stop the baby from crying. The baby becomes terrified further and cries louder. The old lady cries out, 'Cheenu please give the baby to me. Once I feed her, she will be quiet. Cheenu please listen to me. Take your hands off the baby's mouth." Cheenu is in no condition to listen. He presses his hands further on the baby's mouth. He clamps it down harder. The baby's crying stops in a few minutes. This child will never cry again. A life that was just beginning to blossom was sacrificed at the altar of addiction. This little human being who had set out to make its mark in this world was erased from the face of the Earth for ever.

The old lady looks up in shock. Why did the baby stop crying? "Oh my God! What did he do?" Realization dawns on the woman slowly and her eyes become huge like saucers in shock. She begins to cry louder. She beats her chest with the bound arms. "What did you do Cheenu? You killed my baby. By killing her, you have killed us. You have killed us all. How are Venkat and Priya going to bear this? What will I tell them?"

Cheenu looks up startled at her. His anger increases ten-fold. "Shut up old woman. It is Venkat's mistake. He should not have gone to the police." He looks around for something to hurt her. He goes to the next room. He locates a broken metal pipe on the floor. He picks up the pipe which is heavy and brings it back with him. He hits very hard on the woman's head. She falls to the floor with a loud thud. The sound of her skull cracking makes Cheenu puke. He rushes into the bathroom and throws up into the sink. He comes back into the room.

The old lady is moaning in pain. Her moaning becomes softer and softer and slowly ceases for ever. A woman who came to participate in the birth of her grandchild became a witness to her death and lost her life in the process. Had she bade farewell to her home land when she left her country of birth? Did she know that she will never see her family again? Did her husband and children know that the journey to London would be her last? Cheenu is satisfied "There, you don't have to answer them anymore. Old fool of a woman, why did she annoy me like this?"

Cheenu looks around him. The drug in his system is wearing off slowly. There is blood everywhere. He justifies his activity by blaming Venkat. "Venkat did this to you. The sin of your death rests on him." He speaks to the corpse. He walks around the room for a while. He sits down beside the lady for a while. He looks at her for a long time. He begins to laugh. A sarcastic laugh and then slowly the laugh becomes a moan and then it transforms into a cry. A slow whine of self pity. He sits for a while and looks at his options. He comes to a decision. He removes the jewellery from the baby's body and then from the old woman and keeps them in his pocket. His shirt is soiled and dirty.

After a long time, he gets up and looks around again. He cleans up everything. A curtain of silence falls in that room which is only disturbed by the cleaning up operation that Cheenu was undertaking. He erases all the evidence of their presence in the room. He is completely sober now. He leaves the room spick and span. He goes outside the warehouse. The sun blinds his eyes and he cannot tolerate its brilliance. His world has become dark. His conscience is bloodied. A weakness of the mind became a wrongful strength for the body. Two lives taken, a whole family destroyed.

THE DECEPTION

Cheenu goes to the poker club. He sits on the bar stool and orders a drink. He is in a lot of tension and he is sweating profusely. His phone rings suddenly and he jumps up from his stool in surprise. He looks at the display on the mobile. Venkat's mobile number appears on the screen. Cheenu screws his face in distaste. "Hello Venkat?"

Venkat speaks in a broken voice, "Cheenu, someone has kidnapped my baby and my mother-in-law." Cheenu is quite for a while. He does not know how to respond. He modulates his voice to feign surprise "Venkat, are you serious. When did this happen?"

Venkat replied, "This morning. She had gone out for her usual walk and did not return home. Priya found a ransom note in the house."

Cheenu sympathises. "I am so sorry Venkat. Do you want me to come over. Do you need any help? Have you informed the police?" Venkat replied, "The police are here and investigating already." So Venkat did call the Police. He did not need any more proof. Venkat deserves it. But now the police are involved. A shiver runs down Cheenu's spine. Someone just walked over his grave. He had not realised the precariousness of his situation until now.

Venkat is wondering at Cheenu's lack of response. "Cheenu! Cheenu! Are you there?" Cheenu comes out of his reverie. "Uh-uh, yes I am here. I am sorry. I was thinking who could have done this? Do you have any enemies?" Venkat is annoyed. "Cheenu. why are you speaking like this? Why would I have enemies? We live a very peaceful life. We never did anyone any harm. Look I have to make a few more phone calls and make more enquires."

Venkat hangs up the phone. Cheenu puts his phone back into his shirt pocket. He is deep in thought now. What will become of him now? He needs to escape. He needs to leave the country. He does not have the money to buy a ticket. He is stupid. He laughs at himself now. He might as well turn himself in. Him leaving the country in a hurry will be a confession of his guilt. They will not need any further proof. He thinks deeply into the night. He comes to the conclusion that he will have to stay. He will be fine. No one will be suspicious of him. They will not discover the bodies. The ware house has been empty for so long.

The warehouse is bathing in the sunshine but is drowning in the wail of the siren from the police cars, the ambulances and the fire engine. The whole place is surrounded by police vehicles and people. A 'do-not-cross' tape is hanging around the periphery of the building. Detective Dev has arrived at the scene. He asks a lady police officer to come close by. "That guy over there was the one who discovered the bodies. The constable is taking down notes of his account of the discovery."

Dev asked if the victims family has been informed? Brenda replied, "Yes, they are on their way." Dev moves into the building and Brenda follows him close behind. Dev is looking around the building. He turns around and looks at Brenda. "I want all the details at my table asap. Ask whoever was dealing with the kidnapping, to report to my office immediately." Brenda agrees, "Yes sir." Dev is a bit more polite now. "Thanks Brenda."

Priya and Venkat are escorted into the crime scene. They are stunned at what they see in front of their eyes. Priya whimpers in pain. She is rearing to go to her daughter and her mother. But she is being restrained by Brenda. Venkat turns around to Priya with tears in his eyes. He holds Priya closely. The events of the last twenty-four hours have aged him by twenty years. Priya is in a disheveled state. Dev observes them minutely. He can see their grief. So genuine that his heart aches at their loss. He orders himself to stay focussed and be objective. Emotions will not get the job done. A clear head and gallons of coffee will.

Dev goes over to his office. The sight that he has seen lingers in front of his eyes. The scene may look clean but the crime is gruesome. Two vulnerable people-one young and one old. Both helpless and limited in their own way-have been victimised. Their life has been stolen from them. The person who is responsible will definitely be brought to justice. He will receive a slow painful punishment. He will have so much free time that he can reflect on his deed for ever!

The police officer who was dealing with the kidnap was waiting for him in the office. He begins to speak and explains everything that took place in the last twenty-four hours. Dev listens to everything in silence. "I will keep this file for the time being. I will call you when I need to speak to you further." Police Officer replies, "Yes sir." He walks to the end of the room, opens the door, salutes, exits and closes the door behind him.

Dev is already deep in thought. He does not need to look at the photos anymore. He has photographic memory. He has heard what he needs to hear. Now he will carry out his own investigation. No time to waste. He gets into his car and drives to the cemetery. He parks the car as explained by the previous officer and does exactly what was explained to him. He takes photos with his camera as he goes along. Then he walks over to Barbara Kendall's grave.

Why did he choose this grave? What is so particular about this position? The tombstone is at an angle to the actual grave. Venkat can wedge the bag in between the two so the bag will not be discovered easily. That is the reason why he chose this spot. Is there any other reason? He looks around. The whole perimeter was surrounded by trees. He could have hidden just anywhere. But he needed to and may have been nearby.

A few meters away in one corner, there was a clump of trees. A private seating area if you wanted to stay and mourn for a little while. Sure he would not have chosen that place to wait and watch? He will be seen. Even though Venkat may not know that the person seated there was the kidnapper; but he will pay attention. He has the need to keep the money safe till the perpetrator got it. If Venkat had to go to the police for some reason, he will have mentioned and described that person first.

The clump of oak trees make a very thick canopy. A person who is lying low and properly camouflaged will not be discovered quickly. Can the person see clearly from there? He will just have to check it out won't he? Dev slowly made his way over to the trees. He looked around for clues as he went. There were cigarette butts all along the path that led to the tree. Different kinds-a testimony to the fact that the place was used frequently. Equal to finding a needle in a haystack! The trees were his best bet. The clue lies in those trees. Dev reached the seating area. He sat down and behaved like a casual visitor. He sat there for a while and observed the whole perimeter. Slowly he raised his head and looked up. He gazed at the tree for a good while. He comes to a conclusion. He gets up from there and drives away.

Dev goes back to the crime scene again. Two police constables are guarding the place. He goes near. The police constables stop him from entering the premises. PC1, Tim speaks to him, "Excuse me sir, you are not allowed to come in here." Dev smiles and displays his ID Tim apologises "Sorry sir, I am new here. I have not met you before." He opens the gate providing entry to Dev.

Dev reassures them. "It is all right officer. It is better to be safe than to be sorry. What is your name?" Tim replies, "My name is Tim and he is Tom." Dev looks at both of them and smiles. "Tim you come with me. Tom you stay guard here." Tom salutes him. Tim walks a few steps behind Dev. They both go into the room where the murder was committed. Dev scrutinises every nook and corner. Tim watches his every move carefully. Dev then goes into the toilet and looks around. The light is turned on. He switches off the light and shines his pen torch. The torchlight gives a better glow, a focal point to pay attention and illuminates the place further.

Tim asks, "Is everything all right sir?" Dev is looking around and he peeps into every corner. He looks behind the cistern and sees something that is slender. Dev with a smile in his voice "Yes, perfectly all right now." He takes a photograph of the object in its original position. He tries to pick up the object with his gloved hand. He is not able to reach it with his fingers.

He looks around to find something which will help him retrieve the object. Eventually he uses his pen torch to try and slide it to the floor. The light from the pen torch moves around like a pendulum in the darkness in his attempt to retrieve the object. After a few attempts he succeeds.

The object falls to the floor. It is a syringe. He picks it up and looks at it closely. There is blood in the syringe. The blood seems to be not fresh but not very old. He secures it in a specimen bag. Dev looks around further. He does not see anything else that raises his suspicion. He walks back outside. "Okay Tim, let's go. We are done for the night." They both come down to the entrance of the building where Tom is standing guard.

Dev says, "Right boys. Keep watch." They both salute Dev acknowledges their salute and walks back to the car. Once seated inside, he turns on the ignition and drives down the street. His mind is full of questions. The ransom note explains the kidnapping but why this family? There are so many families in this country who are richer and yet more accessible. The spoilt rich kids can be actually led by their nose into a trap and there will be no trouble to obtain the ransom.

Their parents will not hesitate to pay. They know that if the police start digging, they will find more skeletons in their closet. It was easier to pay than have the police snooping around their business. Venkat did go to the graveyard and keep the bag as directed. Then why kill the small baby and the old lady? Well, he has to wait for the answers.

At the moment his brain is not co-operating. What he needs is; good food and a bottle of beer. Once his tummy is full, his brain will be energised and refuelled. He pulls out the mobile phone from his pocket and orders food. He then drives to the office and goes into the darkroom where he begins to develop the photos. Once that is done, he hangs them out to dry. He is tempted to look at them while they are still wet. But he schools himself and comes out of the dark room. His food has arrived and is on the table. He rubs his hands together. He had not realised how hungry he was. He tucks into his food with gusto and once he has finished eating, he resumes his work.

He is in a better frame of mind now and can concentrate better. The events of the whole day had left a sadness in his heart. The psychology of the human mind and its relationship to greed and the subsequent desperation was the reason for most of the crimes. It is the personal nature of the person which decides whether it gruesome or not.

This person did not torture them but he is not a good person. Even if he was desperate, he should not have chosen the two most vulnerable group of people. A young baby and an old woman. People who need to be supported and nurtured in unique ways were deliberately chosen to meet his selfish ends. This is definitely a man's job. A woman however cruel will not do this to a small baby. There have been incidences of womb snatching where the women are killed for the babies but the babies are loved and cherished. No, this is definitely a man!

He gets up to make coffee. He visits the loo while he is waiting for the coffee to percolate. When he returns, the whole room is wafting with the aroma of the coffee. Thank God for coffee! The best cure for hangover and tiredness alike. A knock is heard on the door. Dev looks up and smiles. Brenda! punctual as ever. The door opens and Brenda walks in. She keeps a file on the table. "Good morning Brenda. Sit down. I will get you some coffee."

Brenda replies, "Thank you Detective. The coffee you make is always good and strong." Dev hands her the coffee and sits down. Brenda hands him the file and he begins to read through it. The sound of the clock rhythmically ticking away the time is the only noise that emanates from the room. Brenda finishes her coffee and waits patiently.

She knows her boss' style. You are not allowed to speak till he is good and ready. Brenda smiles to herself. She has made him sound like a puppeteer. He is a good man and a fair boss. She looks around the room. The photo of his partner is the centre piece on top of the fireplace. A very beautiful woman. Brenda is startled from her thoughts by the sound of Dev's chair scraping on the floor. "Come on Brenda, let's go." Brenda quickly gathers her stuff and walks hurriedly out after Dev.

Venkat and Priya are sitting on the sofa and Dev and Brenda are seated on comfortable chairs across from them. Dev extends his condolences. "Mr. Venkat, we are sorry to disturb you at such a sad time. I hope you understand that we have to ask you a few questions to help us obtain some answers. Nobody can bring your loved ones back but your answers will help us catch the murderer sooner."

Priya begins to sob and Venkat holds her close. Dev continues, "So you are Mr. Venkat and this is your wife Priya?" Venkat says, "Yes that is correct." "You both are working", Dev makes a neutral statement. Venkat murmurs. Dev asks. "Do you suspect anyone?" Venkat replies, "No. I have only very few friends here and they all know my family and my family knows them."

Dev prods further, "Do you have any enemies?" Venkat replies in the negative. Dev thinks in a different angle, "Did you let any strangers inside recently? You know Plumber, electrician any one?" Venkat shook his head, "No. The house is newly built."

Another angle from Dev: "Did your mother-in-law know any one other than your friends? Your original report says that your mother-in-law used to go for walks with your baby. Did she make any acquaintances on her daily walk?"

Venkat is frustrated. "No, she did not know anyone other than our friends. She doesn't know the language that's why she never spoke to anyone outside the house. Most of my friends speak our language and so she was able to communicate with them." Dev asks him if he was sure. Venkat is definite, "Yes, I am positive. In fact she was so lonely here that she used to recite every small detail from her daily walks. It was our baby that was keeping her here. Otherwise she would have gone home ages ago."

Dev asked if he could repeat everything that happened on the day they were kidnapped? Dev looks at Brenda. She has already been taking notes. She knows that her senior has a particular style of working. He gets the job done perfectly and he closes the loop so well that no perpetrator can wriggle out of it. Venkat answers with a big sorrowful sigh, "On the day, she rang me at ten o clock to say that she was going for her usual walk." Dev interrupts. "Does she go everyday or-?"

Venkat continues, "She goes if it is not raining. Our daughter would not let her sit at home." He smiles at the thought and then his smile gives way to sorrow and a wetness in his eyes. Priya sees this and begins to cry again. Brenda hands her a paper towel which Priya takes with thanks. She wipes her eyes and keeps it in her fist. Brenda extends her palm and Priya hands the hand towel over. Brenda keeps the hand towel back into her bag.

Venkat observes this but says nothing. They are doing their job. However painful it may be to his wife and him. They had to go through the motions. The immediate family was always the primary suspect. He answered, "She never went too far as she did not know the places well. She will usually not go any further that the next two blocks. Sometimes she will go to the supermarket on the Main Street. She did not know the route to the other places."

Dev looks at Priya "Priya, this is the letter you received from the kidnapper. Mm--what time does the postman usually arrive?" Priya replies, "He usually comes around 10:30 am. Dev asks, "So then what happened?" Venkat continued, "I rang her around half ten as they will have finished half of their walk. She will usually return at 11 in time to prepare lunch. She used to feed Aishu fresh home cooked hot meals everyday." Again Venkat's throat gets wet and Priya sniffles.

Venkat holds her close. "She will ring me at 11 when she has returned. Then Priya will ring her at 1pm. So that day she did not answer my call or ring me at 11 so I rang her again. But the phone seemed to be switched off. I thought that the battery was probably out of charge." Dev looked at him encouraging him to continue.

Venkat gets some confidence. He thinks to himself, "This man, in-spite of his rough exterior has a soft corner. He does understand them." He continued to speak, "Then Priya rang me at 1pm. Her mother had not answered her call either. She thought that may be I was speaking to her so I told her everything and asked her to go home to see if everything was okay".

Detective looked at Priya and she took up from there. She narrated the events as they occurred. When she finished speaking, the room was enveloped in silence. Priya's sobs echoed in the quiet room. After giving her an opportunity to vent her grief, Dev continues "If you don't mind, could we see some pictures of your family and friends?" "Yes sure" Venkat goes into the bedroom and comes out with a picture album.

The four of them sit at the table and Venkat begins to show them the pictures. "These pictures are from Aishwarya's naming ceremony. This is my mother-in-law with my daughter. She looked so different this morning. A contrast to the lively woman that she was until yesterday." Priya's cry becomes louder at the memory of her mother's corpse.

Venkat leans towards Priya's chair and hugs her close to him. Detective Dev and Assistant Brenda do not speak. Silence was the only form of communication that was best suited for this moment. Venkat slowly turns the pages of the album; giving them a chance to look at the photos properly. Venkat continues, "This is the four of us again. These here are my friends Swaraj, Rupesh, Sarvanan, Mukil and Sanjay. They were here with their families. This here is Cheenu. He is a bachelor. These are my other colleagues from my office. These are Priya's colleagues and her boss. He turns another page: "These are my neighbors. This is my boss and his wife."

He hands the album to Detective. Detective looks at the photos again. He then looks at Venkat. Can I keep this album for some time? I will return it to you when the investigation is finished. Venkat agrees. "Yes, but please can I have the first photo that I showed you-of my mother-in-law and our daughter? We have to initiate customs according to our culture. Priya does not have the emotional strength to do it. One of my friend and his family have offered to come and do it for us."

Dev nods. "Yes, we understand. Is that the only photo you need? There are other photos?" Venkat is definite. "No, that is the only proper photo of them together. They died together. I don't want to separate them even in the picture." Priya sobs harder. Dev thanks them. "Thank you for tolerating us so far. Is it okay if we look around the rooms and get an understanding of your life?" Venkat does not see the need but he concedes. "Y--yes that is fine?"

Dev walks into the first adjacent room which is the kitchen. Venkat follows him close behind. Brenda completes the trio. Priya just stays there on the sofa and is gazing far away. Her thoughts are with her mother and her baby. Detective Dev looks around the kitchen. The place is scrupulously clean. No cooking has been done. Dev looks at Venkat and asks, "Did someone clean this kitchen? It is very clean."

Venkat replied, "My mother in law before she left for the walk." Venkat sobs. "'She used to clean the kitchen three times a day and the house in the morning and the evening. Mop the house every Tuesday and Thursday-a custom from our country."

Detective Dev opens the presses and looks at the contents. No processed food, nothing that was ready to eat. Every ingredient needed to cook a meal from scratch was there. Fully stocked cupboard. The family lived a healthy lifestyle. It looked like they could afford it. Well, between the two of them working, they could afford good food and the naming ceremony also was very grand. Might have attracted someone else's unwanted attention as well. There were only about fifty people for the ceremony and that was including the families of the friends. Nearly all of them were Indians. Very few locals! Just the neighbors and the boss, Not a huge list to work on.

They next walk into the master bedroom. It was a total contrast from the calmness of the kitchen. A very evident sign of the mother-in-law not being there. Signs of having had a disturbed night. Cushions all over the floor. The couch moved to face the window. That was definitely Priya. Waiting for the two people; she loved the most in the world to come back. A helpless Venkat lying on the bed urging her to lie down for a few hours. It was not working. She had not moved from that position. The amount of soiled hand towels were a testimony to the night's vigil.

Brenda could have easily picked one of these; had she known. But the sample of tissue that she got from Priya will be a concrete evidence to absolve her. There was a sealed envelope on the table with the   receivers address written on it. Probably a birthday card to someone in India. It maybe for a niece or a nephew. Well, there won't be any celebrations for a year now as per their custom. Deeply entrenched in religion, the whole community sans religion came together as a family in the time of a person's need. There is a huge lesson to be learnt from them. Unity in Diversity!

Detective Dev looked at Venkat and asked him, "May I get a glass of water if it is not a hassle?" Venkat is apologetic. "anywaySorry we cannot offer you tea as we won't be cooking until after the funeral." Dev looked at Venkat in surprise. Venkat shrugs and replies, "We won't feel hungry anyway. It is in our culture that when a family member dies; we do not cook anything until after we come back from the graveyard ." Dev nodded his head in understanding. His heart bled for the young couple. So much in love and so much more in grief!

Venkat goes out into the kitchen. Detective Dev quickly picks up the letter from the table and slips it into his coat pocket. He takes a few photos of the room. He then turns around in time to see Venkat coming back into the room with a glass of water. He picks up a pen from his pen-case and accidentally drops it onto the floor. Venkat hands the glass of water to Dev and bends to the floor to pick up the pen. He hands the pen to Dev who looks at both his hands and then apologetically at Venkat. Venkat understands that Dev's both hands are busy and keeps the pen back into the pen-case. That was Dev's intention. To get a fingerprint from Venkat.

Dev thanks him, drinks the water, and then closes the pen-case. He puts the pen-case back into his pocket. They then proceed to the smaller bedroom that was shared by Aishwarya and her grandmother. A few more minutes of inspection and they leave the house with assurances to Venkat and Priya. Before leaving, Brenda asks him to sign a form of consent for removing their property, the picture album from them. Venkat signs without any hesitation. Brenda looks at the signature closely. Does not resemble the handwriting on the envelope. At least they have got their handwriting sample which will help to rule them out. One could see their grief which upheld their innocence but evidence is needed for their acquittal.

Venkat receives a phone-call. He looks at the caller id. Cheenu of all people. Venkat in a sober voice, "Hello Cheenu, how are you?" Cheenu replies, "Venkat, I am fine; but I wanted to find out if the two of you were ok. Can I do something for you? Can I buy some food and come?

I don't know to cook otherwise I would have offered to cook."

Venkat replies. "No Cheenu! We are not hungry. I don't think we will ever feel hungry again." Cheenu sympathises: "Venkat, you are very upset at the moment. How is Priya?" Venkat retorts. "How can she be? She is a mother. A part of her body and soul has been wrenched of her."

Cheenu is hasty in his response. "I know, I am sorry. May be you should go somewhere. Go to a seaside resort for a few days. Surely the police will not mind that?" Venkat sighed. "It will be good to go Cheenu. But the police asked us not to leave the city. They are continuing their investigation." Cheenu asks, "Do they know who is behind all of this? Venkat replied to his query, " No they are still investigating. It's not that easy."

Cheenu hurriedly, "Yeah sorry I know. I just want to know who can be this cruel.

Killing a small baby and an old lady. I am going to get off the phone now. Please let me know if you need something." Venkat thanks him. "No, we are fine. Thanks." Cheenu bids farewell. "Okay bye."

Cheenu reflects deeply on the phone call. The police are looking but they do not have someone to put the blame on--Yet. He needed to get away from here. But where can he go. He had no money or a place to go to. Why did Venkat have to go to the police? Things would have ended up so much more differently if he had not done so.

AVENGING PROSPERITY

The same day, Detective Dev and Assistant Brenda went over to Venkat's neighbourhood. They enquired to the neighbors and asked them some questions. Brenda gave each one of them a piece of paper to write their name, address and contact numbers and to sign the consent to be contacted if necessary. Everyone was sympathetic and complied. They were in love with the baby and the grandmother was a cheerful kind. She would keep to herself but only because of the language barrier.

Dev and Brenda leave the neighbourhood and visit each of Venkat's friends. They repeat the process there and also visited Priya's and Venkat's office. After making enquiries everywhere, they go back to their office. Detective Dev and Assistant Brenda are standing near the table in Dev's room. The whole table is covered with evidence, photos, reports, statementsreport-**B**, etc. The whiteboard is full of algorithms.

Shoe imprint 5' 5"or 6' (Plaster of Paris copy of the shoe imprint).

Blood sample report-**B** Negative

Used syringe-**B** Negative

Vomit - Same DNA as the blood

Urine specimen - Same DNA as the blood

CCTV footage: A man 5'5" in height, head covered by a hood for the winter, side profile to the camera-has staked out the warehouse and knows it like the back of his hand. The buggy being pushed by the man, the woman walking in willingly means that the person is known to them. Narrows the group down to close friends.

Hair samples on the pipe-from the female.

Blood samples on the pipe from the female.

Photos from the murder scene, Suggests only a mild struggle.

Photos from the cemetery

Ransom note

Something was very off about the ransom note. Obviously it was not signed but something else. If they could not find anything from all this, they were back to square one What did the note say? What is so different? 'Venky Yes that's it' His name is Venkat. So why Venky? Was that a term of endearment? Dev immediately dials Venkat's number on his mobile. Venkat looks at the unknown number and answers. "Hello." Dev replies, "Venkat this is Detective Dev. Is it a good time to ask you a few questions if it is all right? Venkat agrees, "Yes officer." Dev asks, "What does Venky mean?" Venkat exclaims, "That is a pet name of my name or a short form of my name."

Dev is silent for a few nanoseconds. "I see. Who calls you Venky?" Venkat replies, "My friends." Dev queries: "All your friends?" Venkat said, "No, Four of my friends call me by that name. Why?" Dev mildly replies. "No, I am just curious. Keep this quiet okay?" Venkat quickly says, "Oh okay. Did you find the person?" Dev reassures him. "Soon Venkat. Very soon"

Dev probes further. "Tell me those friends names." Venkat calls out their names and then he hangs up. Brenda looks at Dev. "What did you find?" Dev grins happily. "Yes, Brenda we are closing in. Some more work. We have to lay a trap now."

Dev looks at the time. "It is already midnight. There is a few more hours work left. Do you want to go home?" Brenda declines, "No, I am learning valuable skills from you. My husband knows that I won't be coming home till we catch the culprit." Dev is hungry. "Okay then. I am going to order food while you continue your work. The usual okay for you?" Brenda thanks him and is in agreement. "Yes, Dev, the usual is good."

Dev walks out with his phone and calls his partner. He speaks to her for a few minutes. Then he orders food from a nearby restaurant. When he comes back, he finds Brenda working away at the computer. The food arrives in a short while. They both love Chinese food. As usual Brenda quickly reaches for the first 'Fortune Cookie'. 'YOUR VENTURE WILL BE SUCCESSFUL' Dev reaches for the second one. He reads it out aloud: 'YOUR FAME WILL CONTINUE' Brenda whines: "Why do I always get the less nice ones? Dev teases her. "That is because you are greedy."

Brenda agrees. "Kevin says the same thing. I don't know why but I just like to get the first one." Dev argues. "First does not necessarily mean the best?" Brenda sighs "Yes I know. Its just that I can't bear to be second. Not if I can help it." Dev surmises. "That is the downside of the profession. You are working in a field that is male dominated." Brenda shrugs her shoulder. She knows that Dev is correct and her competitive streak is stronger because of her chosen profession.

They have their dinner at a side table and Brenda goes back to continue typing after dinner. Dev clears all the papers on the desk one by one and files them away neatly. Only four photos and their consent form in their own handwritings remain. He matches them one by one with the Ransom note. Rupesh-No! Saravanan-No! Mukil-No! Cheenu-No.! Dev's happy bubble bursts very quickly. He looks at all the four consent forms again and again. He looks up at Brenda. She is fast asleep on her chair. Dev smiles to himself. "She works very hard. She does not have his strength." Glad that she cannot read his mind.

She is a feminist to the very core. She will stand as long as the last man stands and possibly longer out of sheer determination. He knows that she did not like what he said earlier on. If it was Kevin who had said it; she would have scratched his eyes out. The poor man. It is only with him that she behaves as a human being. Only because they are school friends and have known each other for a long time.

Well, to get back to work! Reminiscing will not get the job done. It is already two am. Time for a cup of coffee. Dev turns on the percolator and takes a stretch. It has been a very long day. By the looks of it, it will be a long night as well. He walks around the table a few times just to get his circulation going. Then he begins to look at the signed papers again. He checks it out with his hand held lens.

He begins a new sheet. He writes a few notes on it. Now he begins to write a new paragraph with his left hand. He repeats exactly what he had written with his right hand. He looks at both the hand writing through the hand lens. Yes, he can see that the way he carves his 'n' with his left hand is the same as with his right hand. Yes, that is the clue. Probably the kidnapper wrote it with a different hand. He was not stupid. He knew that the ransom note will be scrutinised. So he has used a different hand to write the note. He now looks at all the notes again. Again and again! One note and then the next. Compare with the ransom note. Yet another paper and checks again. His eyes begin to water. He looks up at the time - 5 am. He even forgot to drink his coffee. Finally he decides to exclude two of the notes. He is definite that those two are not the culprit.

He looks at the third note again and keeps it aside. He wonders who of these two people could it be? Wait! Dev consults his notes again. The third person was not in the city on the day. He had gone to Birmingham to meet his extended family. His alibi was checked and found correct. The local police in Birmingham had confirmed his presence in the city for twelve hours before and after. He then looks at the fourth note. He keeps looking at it for a good while. He is definite. This is the person. But he needs DNA evidence to prove the actual perpetrators guilt. He will be happier with a confession but first things first.

He looks up at the clock. 6 am-The day time crew will be here shortly. He gets up and goes to the window. He opens the window and breathes in the fresh air for a few minutes. He then gives a large yawn. All the cobwebs from his body get blown away. He fills the percolator with fresh water from the water dispenser. The coffee is tastier when made with filtered water and just a few degrees less than the boiling point. Not mineral water though. Then he goes to the restroom to wash his face. He comes out and pours the coffee into two mugs. One he leaves at his side of the desk.

He then walks up to Brenda. "Brenda coffee" Brenda wakes up with a start. She sees Dev standing in front of him with a coffee mug. She grins sheepishly. "Sorry, what time is it." Dev smiles. "Time for the rooster to crow and the crew to walk in." Brenda thanks him. "Okay, I will freshen up."

She takes the coffee mug from his hand and sips it. Fresh energy runs through her veins. She keeps the coffee mug on the table. "I will be ready in five minutes" and walks into the rest room. Two minutes later, Brenda comes out of the restroom. She is looking fresh now. Tired but presentable.

Dev gets up from his chair and puts on his coat. Brenda gathers all the files and walks beside him. The crew are all gathered in the conference room. The details from the Whiteboard in Dev's

Office has been fed into the projector of the conference room. All the members of the Tactical Support Team were present. Dev scrutinised each person intently. The 'Trojans' were alert and ready to move on their team leaders command. Their team leader was William who was fondly known as Billy.

"Good morning ladies and gentlemen" Dev held eye contact with each one of them. They were all in good spirits. There was no guarantee as to what the perpetrator was like. Well, he was a double murderer! He had committed an Infanticide and a homicide. He will not hesitate to kill again. The motive was the desperate need for money. Money to feed his addiction. His desperation will have increased when he saw the police in the cemetery. He surely will have realised that the people present there were the police. He was there all the time-watching and waiting. The police did not check thoroughly. He could have been caught the same day before he had done any real harm. The police are as responsible as Cheenu. When Cheenu realised that the police are involved, he got angry. It was in anger and spite that he killed them. The spite gained more fuel from the drug in his system. He will not stop at anything. "The boys have to be very careful." These men and women will not hesitate to kill or die but their families needed them back. When they say goodbye to their loved one's every morning, they know that it might be the last 'goodbye' or 'love you' or any other endearment they may say to their families. Wether it is the Military, Navy, Airforce or the Police. Their life is the same. If you see them after they come back from an operation; they are yours. Their families live in a state of constant anxiety and hope.

Cheenu's photo was centre piece on the whiteboard. His details including his height, weight, employment details, the reason for his crime--- every single detail about him was written on the board. Dev and Brenda had left no stone unturned.

Even the crew could see that this person
will be convicted. The public prosecutor
will see to that. But they had to get him
first. Dev filled them with all the details
and then Billy took over. The roadmap
and the compound of Clive's Poker Club,
the perpetrator's house, his place of
employment were all displayed in
different sections of the whiteboard now.
Billy gave orders to his team regarding
their sequence of raid, their positions and
their tasks in each operation and their
code commands. Dev inspires confidence.
"Bring him back alive boys." They all
salute in unison and file out of the room.
This operation that was called 'Avenging
prosperity' (Getting Justice for Aishwarya)
was under way now. Cheenu had stopped
talking. It is midday by now and the room
was very quiet.

Dev does not relent. "What did you do
with the jewellery?" Cheenu bowed his
head in shame. "I kept them safe in my
apartment?" Dev persists. "Where?"
Cheenu replied, "It is in my suitcase."
Dev is out for blood now. "Are you now

sorry that you did this?" Cheenu looked at him and said, "Yes and no." Dev probed, "Can you explain."

John jumps up. He knew that this was going to go against Cheenu. Even if he did not agree with what Cheenu had done, it was his job to keep him safe. "That's enough. You have got a confession. You have to disregard the last question. Is that understood?" Dev turns off the tape-recorder after completing the formalities. Cheenu is walked back to his holding cell by one of the deputies. John gets up and takes a stretch. He goes out for a smoke.

Dev and Brenda look at each other. "What do you think Brenda?" She replies, "We have got a confession as we had hoped. John can still contest it and get a reduced sentence." Dev agrees. "Our job was to get him. We did that. The rest is up to the Jury to decide. John will have probably left by now. Can you check what is the nearest date that we can get from the Magistrates Court?"

Brenda is eager to do that. "I will do that now. I don't think it will be any soon; but I will try and get the earliest date possible." Dev gave a big sigh. "It will still have to go to the Crown Courts. It won't be over soon." Brenda looked at him pointedly "What is wrong Dev? This is not like you to be so impatient?" Dev with a sad smile "Don't worry. I am not getting involved. It is because it was a very small helpless child who got killed." Brenda sadly said, "Yes I know but we need to remain objective."

Dev suddenly smiled, "You know; Lily thinks that you are the best person I got for a junior. She says that you keep me on the straight and narrow while I am at work." Brenda laughed. "And she does that when you get home. You have no where to drown your misery or to hide." With that retort, Brenda walked out of the office with her mobile pressed to her ear. She smiled on hearing her husband's sweet and loving voice.

The Portobello market street is full of vendors. They have laid out their wares categorically in neat piles under colorful canopies. Kiosks are churning out hot tea, coffee and tasty ethnic food. The stalls on either side of the street are selling tasty street foods from different countries. The truffles, jellies, sugar candies, peanut balls all provided a colorful feast to the eyes. There is an Arabic shop which has exotic chandeliers, music tapes, pipes, incense sticks, perfumes, ornamental decorations, figurines and cigars on display.

The Indian curio shop next doors is full of statues, incense sticks and holders to burn them in, traditional herbal medicines, henna cones, colorful rugs, blankets and sheets, utensils, artefacts , etc. Priya is walking around the shop collecting the stuff for her mother and daughter's month minder. She buys vermillion, incense sticks, oil lamps and plastic flower leis. She goes over to the fruit stall to buy banana, apples, oranges and dates. Those were her mothers favourite fruits. Her eyes clouded over with grief. It has been a month since they both died. "My poor baby and my poor mother. Why did he do it?"

A newspaper boy shouts from the street corner which attracts her attention "Hot news! Hot news! The double murder case is coming to the magistrate courts tomorrow." All the people gather around him. They all start talking loudly. All the people, nationals and expatriates are angry. It is a double murder. The murder of a child is so gruesome that people are filled with hate for this guy. Priya's legs become heavy as if they are set in stone. She cannot move her legs. She wants to reach the paper boy but, she has no strength left. Suddenly she sways like a slender grass in the fields which sways hither and thither in the strong wind. As she is about to fall, an arm goes around her. "Priya are you ok?" Venkat's face swims into Priya's vision. "Venkat, the paper boy! The paper boy!"

Venkat replied softly. "Yes, I know baby. I heard him. That is why I came running to see if you were ok".Priya leaned into him, "I am glad that you came. I was about to fall. I could not move my legs. I wanted to go near him and hear what he was saying. My legs just would not carry me." Venkat squeezes her hand. "I am glad that you did not go. We know that it is happening tomorrow. We will go to the Magistrate's court. We will have to! Is the pain of our baby and your mother's death not enough? Do we have to listen to what the media are saying about it?" Priya weakly smiles "No I suppose not. I just could not stop myself." Venkat tugs at her hand, "Let's go home. Did you buy everything that we need for the pooja tomorrow?" Priya replied, "Yes, I did." Venkat pulled her. "Let's go then."

Next morning, Priya and Venkat get into their car and drive to the magistrates court. Their friends will be there to support them. The neighbors have made placards written with 'Justice for Aishwarya,' 'Justice for Granny' . They have them attached to their windows, cars, gates and every tree around the estate. They have also decided to go to the court to witness the hearing.

Priya and Venkat reach the court building. Lots of people are gathered at the edge of the streets. They are also holding placards. This case has generated a lot of interest. People have been affected by the gruesomeness of the murder, the victims who were brutally murdered and the reason for the murder. The prison vehicle drives into the court compound. People begin to shout slogans of "baby murderer down! down!". "Baby murderer down! down!". The police were trying very hard to control the crowd who were getting exited at every call of the slogan.

Dev and Brenda drove into the court compound. They walked over to Priya and Venkat and shook their hands with them. Venkat and Priya smiled sadly at them. Dev and Brenda understood their pain. Dev apologetically smiles "I am sorry this is unavoidable and has to be done". Venkat looks at Priya and then straight at Dev "This is the last place we want to be, but we understand." Brenda looks at her watch "Let's go in."

The four of them walk into the court room. Venkat and Priya go and sit at the bench in the front. Dev and Brenda walk to the front half of the court and meet the Public Prosecutor. They shake hands and then they sit down in the bench behind the Public Prosecutor, Alfred Smith. The court is full of people. Venkat and Priya's friends along with their spouses, the neighbors and their partners and Venkat and Priya's bosses all are seated at the back. All have come together in this occasion to express solidarity to Venkat and Priya; when they needed them the most. Cheenu is already seated beside his lawyer, John Noel. He does not look at anyone. He just stares straight ahead. He is cleanly shaved and has worn a tailored suit. The Usher walks into the courtroom and announces "All rise".

Everyone rose from their seats. The three 'Justice' of Peace walked in and took their seats. Then everyone sat down. The chairperson and the wingers read the notes kept in front of them. Priya and Venkat looked closely at the three people, who were going to decide about their daughter and mother's case. One was a French school teacher. He looked like a kind man. The second person was a lady, a Nigerian doctor. She looked motherly despite being career driven. The third man was an English postman. He looked very focussed. Like a person who will get the job done. The three of them work part time as Justice of Peace. They confer with each other for a few minutes and then turn towards the courtroom. The chairperson asks the Public Prosecutor to begin the proceedings. The Public

Prosecutor gets up from his chair "Yes my Worship".

The Public Prosecutor begins his opening speech. 'My Lords, on the day of the 09/11/2017, Mrs Nayagam went out for a walk with her two year old granddaughter Aishwarya in a buggy at around 10 am. She was accosted by Mr. Cheenu, the accused and kidnapped for a ransom of Eighty-Thousand Pounds. Circumstantially the Crown police got involved in the rescue operation. With the help of the Crown Police, Aishwarya's father, Mr. Venkat organised the money and dropped it at the collection point which was a grave of a certain Barbara Kendall in the Kensal Green Cemetery. The couple and the police stayed vigil for most of the night but neither the ransom was collected nor the abducted people returned. Next day the Crown Police discovered the body of the baby and the grandmother at a warehouse some distance away from their house. The forensic pathologist has confirmed the DNA of the deceased with their family member, Mrs. Priya Venkat who is the daughter of the deceased woman and mother to the deceased baby." Priya holds back a chocking cry. Venkat hands her the hand towel over; he had kept it ready in his pocket. He knew that his wife will need it.

The Public Prosecutor then hands over the photographic evidence of the murdered people to the Legal Advisor who hands it to the Chair person. All three Justice of Peace looked at the photo with horror. A few minutes later, the chairperson spoke to the Public Prosecutor "It is evident that a double murder has been committed. Who do you suspect in the murder of this lady and baby?" The Public Prosecutor looked at Cheenu and then at his notes. "Mr. Cheenu who is present at the witness stand has been presented by the Crown Police as the possible culprit."

The chairperson looked at Cheenu. "Do you agree to having committed the crime? Do you plead guilty?" Cheenu squared his shoulder, lifted up his head with pride "No my Worship. I did not commit the crime." The defense attorney gets up from his chair and speaks "My Lord, my client Mr. Cheenu does not plead guilty." The chairperson looked at the defense lawyer "It is all right counsel. Please take your seat."

The three Justice of Peace convene together and then they ask the legal advisor to approach the bench. The legal advisor gets up from his seat and approaches the bench. The four of them confer together and then the legal advisor sits back in his seat. The chairman looks at the accused. 'Mr. Cheenu. you have pleaded not guilty so the case is being passed over to the Crown court. Moreover the seriousness of the offense mandates that you get a fair trial and the victims' family receive proper justice. It is not within the scope of the Magistrate Court to hold this case any further. You will be remanded back into the custody of the crown police till the case comes for hearing in the Crown Court. The case is adjourned." The usher cries, "All rise".

Everyone in the court stand and the Justice of Peace leave the room. The people start chatting amongst themselves and after a lot of scraping of chairs, the court is finally empty. Venkat and Priya also come out into the sunshine but their world is enveloped in darkness. Alfred Smith approached them and held Priya's hand in a gesture of respect. He looked at her in the eyes "I am so sorry that you have to go through all this and more. We had hoped that he will plead guilty and will be indicted in the Crown Court. But he seems to be just stubborn."

Venkat wanted to know, "What will happen next?" The Public Prosecutor explained that the Justice of Peace will refer the case to the Crown Court. They will probably call for a hearing in 6-8 weeks. Venkat then asked, "Will it be all right to go back home to India in the meantime? The police had asked us to not leave the country. Our people back home are very upset and it will do them good to see us. Moreover we cremated our daughter and Priya's mother here. The family did not even get to mourn them properly. We would like to go home and disperse their ashes after offering proper prayers and doing all the necessary ritual".

Alfred indicated to Dev and he walked towards them. Then Alfred turned to Dev "Will it be all right if Mr. and Mrs. Venkat leave the country to go home for a while?" Dev replied, "Of course, we could not let you go sooner as we did not know how today would turn out. We may have needed you to give evidence. Please come back in four weeks time. The case should come for hearing in six weeks at the earliest." Venkat assured him. "Of course we will."

ETERNAL RESTING PLACE

Venkat and Priya landed at Chennai Airport. Landing on the home soil did not generate a feeling of happiness. Priya very lovingly and carefully, picked up the two copper urns; carrying the ashes of her precious daughter and her beloved mother from the overhead cabinet. Another sob escaped her throat. Venkat gathered the hand luggage, gripped her hand tightly and led her through the aisle. The air hostess and the pilot standing at the doorway bade them a sober goodbye. They were aware of what was happening. Dev had ensured to ring the airlines and apprise them of their situation. The airline staff also rose above their level of hospitality and upgraded their tickets to a business class. They also allocated them a private corner seat. Immigration clearance was smooth. They did not have any main luggage. There was no preparation or shopping. No energy left in the two of them. They reached the arrival lounge. The families on both sides were waiting for them. Her father was waiting for her. His sister, her favourite aunt and godmother was there along with the rest of them. She walked, no literally flew into her aunt's arms. Her aunt folded her into her bosom and began to comfort and rock her just as she used to do when Priya was a baby. There was no words. There was no need for words anymore. They held each other for a long time. She found solace in her aunt's arms.

Priya's father stepped over to his son-in-law and hugged him. Venkat also felt a sense of relief. He was carrying a huge burden. The burden of his mother-in-law and daughter's death and Priya's grief. He may not have committed the murder himself but as the patriarch of his small family, he felt the weight of his decision to get his mother-in-law to come to London to stay with them. He found forgiveness in his father-in-law's embrace. After being released from that understanding grasp, he stepped over to his father. He could become a child again, a son and leave all the decision making to the elders of the family. Obviously they will consult him but they had more knowledge of what needed to be done. Tomorrow, there will be the ceremony of the last rites where he and his father-in-law had to step in again. He for his daughter and his father-in-law will complete the rites for his deceased wife, Venkat's mother-in-law. For now he could flow with the tide. He had proper time to grieve for the daughter who he will not be able to hold again. Until now he was carrying the burden of Priya's grief. Now he could think about his own grief. He will not bring his baby out to learn Ballet and Bharat Natyam. He will not be able to hear her sing Classical or rock music. He will not tumble in the grass with her. He will not get to scare her first boyfriend. A boy who thinks he is all grown up but only has a few short bristles to show for a moustache. He knew his daughter would have been a confident and outgoing woman. She would have grown up to be a prodigy. Priya could sing and dance very well. She was an award winner in the local competitions when she was young. She was able to perform her on-stage debut performance 'arangetram' in one of the most eminent dance theatres in Chennai. This is like a graduation in the chosen field of arts. You yourself could not decide to appear for the assessment. Your art teacher, the 'Guru' told you when you were ready. His daughter would have grown up to be like her mother. But all wasted over someone's greed. All destroyed in the tornado of someone's addiction. She will remain a baby forever. Not going through the pain of rearing a child and rejoicing in the tiny little achievements and failures was like a dagger slowly being twisted deeper and deeper into his heart. "Oh my baby, I will miss you so much".

Soberly, the group moved out into the waiting convoy of vehicles. Aishwarya and granny now commenced the last part of their journey in the form of ashes in the copper urns to their eternal resting place. They were going to integrate into the soil, water and air and become part of the environment. Part of the landscape one had really loved and the other had never seen.

Two hours later they reached Priya's ancestral home. The last rites will be conducted here. The house was full of people. Aishwarya and her granny's photos were already reposing in frames in the central courtyard. The picture frames were huge, Vermillion, Turmeric and fresh flowers adorned the frames. A small lamp was lighted in front of the frames.

The relatives who lived far away had already arrived in dribs and drabs. The neighbors and the local community were already present to express their solidarity with the grieving family. The place looked like it was preparing for an occasion but the happiness and cheer that goes with it was not there. In ordinary circumstances Venkat's and Priya's return even for a short holiday would have generated a great amount of joy.

The next day, the central courtyard was converted into a place of worship temporarily. Fire in a square of clay and brick pit called 'Homam' was burning in the middle of the courtyard. The priest also known as the 'Aiyyer' who was contracted for the day; was sitting cross legged on a flat very low wooden stool in front of this fire. He was chanting the Mantra. The holy fire which was kept alive by Camphor, mango wood and Ghee burned with a soft glow. The smell of burning ghee filled the entire house. That's how ancient families worked.

The birth, the wedding, the coming of age for the girl, the completion of religious education for the boy, the wedding, childbirth and eventually the death was celebrated in the central courtyard. The children grew up on the knees of their grandparents in this courtyard. It was their home, school, playground all rolled into one. A person's life began and ended there. For a male it was his own home and for the female it was the house she made with her husband and called it her home.

Life and death occurred when they were surrounded by their families. Not for granny though! She may have been surrounded by her loving family when she was born. She died in a far away country, away from her relatives, in a dirty warehouse, killed by a person in whom she had placed her trust. Does anyone have it written on their foreheads- that they have criminal tendency? That they are actually strangers inside? A person however close they are; no matter however much you think that you know them; there will always be a stranger inside them.

When you live in another country, the people you became acquainted with, became your friends. Then they slowly become involved in your happiness and pain. Then they become very dear to you. They may never become part of the family but they became part of your daily

Clive Dev

lives. They are treated like family. The
relationship will be in par with the
relationship you had with the family
member who was this person's friend.
How do you expect one such person to
turn out to be your family's or your killer?
Man is a social animal and lives by the
rules of the society. Some people cannot
conform to the normal and will have
trouble adjusting but whatever the
difficulty, no one had the right to kill
another human being.

The backyard was full of people as well.
These were the cooks and the assistants.
Big cauldrons on huge furnaces fuelled by
firewood were brimming with food. Their
delicious aroma was filling the air. The
various corners were stocked up with raw
goods on palettes for the preparation of
the meal. Sacks of rice, pulses, vegetables,
basic ingredients for dessert like ghee,
sweet, nuts, flour from various sources
were neatly arranged on top of the
wooden planks on the floor. Large sized
banana leaves were being wiped clean to
be used as traditional plates for eating.

The visiting people; in this case, their entire community and their far flung relatives all needed to be fed. Life and death-both were celebrated with a meal. The time of mourning will be officially over as of today. They will be able to carry on with their lives once the guests leave. The period of mourning was not over for Venkat's and Priya's family. They will miss their loved ones in the fabric of daily living. It was definitely not over for Venkat and Priya. They still had to go back to London and see the case through.

Four weeks later, the same people gathered in the airport departure lounge. There were tears in everyone's eyes. They were trying to be strong for each other but sometimes your emotions rule over your common sense. Priya and Venkat walked over to the emigration desk, got processed and were on the other side. They kept looking backwards towards their families till they turned the corner of the first floor past the security check and could not see them anymore. Wish they could turn the clock back.

The plane landed at Heathrow airport, London uneventfully. London was bathed in the late winter sunshine. There were small signs of the spring waiting in the corner. The crocuses were in full bloom. The Daffodil buds were hanging with their heads down. Waiting patiently for the sun to give the command. Then they will lift their head up in pride and wave gently with the breeze.

Priya and Venkat were oblivious to all of this. The happiness with which she had arrived in this country was not there anymore. Back then, she had held her new husband's hands timidly trying to slow him down so that she could have a good look at the place that was going to be her future home. There was no curiosity anymore. She could not look at the place within that same frame of happiness. They reached their dwelling place. The garden was very tidy. Obviously it was their neighbour Peter. He was the one who had helped them settle into their new house and make it a home.

Strangers Inside

The house was neater. Their friends and family had minded the house well. Aishwarya and granny's photos were removed from the centre of the living room to the shelf relegated to their other deities. The tiny lamp was full of oil and lit. They were adorned with fresh flowers and vermillion. The food was cooked. The fridge was well stocked. All signs of their friends being around and caring for the house. Yet today, they were conspicuous by their absence. Priya and Venkat had their shower and went straight to bed. They were jet-lagged and tired. They had to meet the Public Prosecutor, Alfred Smith tomorrow to commence preparation and training to prepare for their part in the trial.

Cheenu was waiting in the meeting room of the prison. He was seated in a chair. The hand cuff was released. There were two guards posted outside the waiting room. Cheenu had been no trouble to anyone. He had been a model prisoner. No challenges, ate on time, slept on time, completed the tasks that were assigned to him. Read some books during his free time. The only trouble was after five pm. He needed to play poker. Otherwise he will shout and scream. Initially the wardens had no clue as to what was wrong. Slowly they understood and provided him with poker cards. He had to play on his own. Were he allowed to gamble with the other prisoners, he will be in their debt and that will become a big problem! The poker cards helped ease the evenings

Now he was waiting for his lawyer-John Noel. He had decided to retain him as his attorney. He had begun to like him. He was a kind and sympathetic man. Cheenu had no illusions about his feelings for what Cheenu had done. One day he had disclosed that he had two daughters. Obviously he loved them. You could see the pride in his eyes. Cheenu was no fool. He knew what John thought of him. He had asked him outright one day. The reply John gave flummoxed him. "Everyone deserves a chance to be defended. To be argued for regardless of what they had done. Crimes are born of desperation but their severity is affected by the situation, the perpetrator finds himself in. Cheenu, you have a right to be represented. That duty falls on me and I will do my best to extricate you as much as possible. You will not go scot free, you know that! But I will try my level best to get you a reduced sentence". These were John's word.

"Hello Cheenu." Cheenu jolted back from his reverie. "Hello John, you are always on time". "Yep! That's me" John grinned. "So we need to prepare you for the trial. I have picked up a set of clothes from your apartment. See if they are the ones that you wanted".Cheenu looked fleetingly at the clothes. "Yes, they are the ones I had in my mind." John checked his list of things to do. "Oh by the way, your mother rang me asking to speak to you. I was waiting for permission from the authorities to bring the mobile phone in so that you could speak to her." Cheenu becomes very angry at John. He explodes "I told you that I didn't want to speak to her."

John explains to him like he was speaking to his five year old daughter. "Cheenu regardless of what you have done and what you feel that your mother thinks. She is your mother. She has a right to speak to you. Do it for her sake."

Cheenu sighs, "Yes I know that she has forgiven me, I know that regardless of what I have done, she loves me but that is what makes it so difficult. Not one of you has even accidentally asked me why I did it?" John replies patiently. "It's not my place to ask you that. Your mother will not ask you that because it has been done. We cannot go back into the past to correct our mistakes." Cheenu looks far away as if he was trying to mentally conure his mother up. "Yes, I suppose so."

John perks up. "So will you speak to your mother?" He felt delighted just the same as   if he was going to speak to his own mother.   Cheenu yields himself to John's charm. "Yes, I will." Just then the phone rings. John answers the phone. "Hello, yes this is John Noel. Oh hello Mrs Janakhi, I am with your son Cheenu at present. I will pass the phone to him. Just bear with me for a second." John looks at Cheenu. He waits for a few minutes. He knows that Cheenu needs a few minutes. His palms are sweating. Tears well in Cheenu's eyes but he wipes them with a determination. He grabs the phone from John. "Hello". Cheenu's mother answers, "Hello, hello Cheenu is that you?" His mother cries on the phone.

Cheenu is sad. "Yes, mother, it is me. How are you?" His mother asks, "I am fine son. Are you eating properly?" Cheenu gets really annoyed and shouts at his mother "Mother, stop this pretence . Do you not want to ask why I did it?" His mother replies firmly, "No Cheenu, not now. I am coming over. We can have a good long chat like the old times."

Cheenu tells her resolutely, "No Mother, you are not going to come. Daddy needs you at home." His mother persuades him, "Cheenu, you are my son. You need me as well. Aunty will look after daddy." Cheenu is being stubborn. "No mother, even if you come, I will not see you. Your journey will be wasted. You stay with dad. If you insist on coming, I will get off the phone now." His mother placates him. "Okay, Cheenu don't hang up. I will not come if that is what you want."

Cheenu went back to his cell once John had finished with him. He was tired after the preparation for the trial. His conversation with his mother was even more emotionally draining. He was not troubled over what he had done. Just no one giving him the opportunity to explain was what riled him. If Venkat had not gone to the police, this will not have happened. He would have had his debt paid off. He would have gone back home a free man. No cares or no worries. He could have been his mother's golden boy. She would have forced him to marry and settle down. This is good. He will never go back home now. His mother cannot get him married off just because she was ready to be a grandmother!

Cheenu had got more books from the library. He had asked for books from his country. He now had the time to read something from the world he was familiar with. At a young age, you were just expected to learn from your syllabus books and achieve something in life. But by that time, your knowledge of the world was limited to what you had learnt in school. Life's needs took over. The rat race began. It just dictated your actions for the rest of your life.

Foot steps could be heard outside Cheenu's cell. The prison warden came near Cheenu's cell. "Mr. Cheenu. you have a visitor." Cheenu is surprised, "I have a visitor! I am not expecting John to come today." The warden smiles, "If John is a female then this probably is John." Cheenu thought a female! "Did

she say what her name was?" The
Warden replied, "Her name is Hema."
Cheenu to himself: Hema! She belonged
to another lifetime.

The Warden handcuffed Cheenu's
extended hands. Then he opened the cell
door. Cheenu followed him out to the
visitor's lobby. Hema was sitting there on
one of the chairs. She looked as beautiful
as ever. Hema looked up and saw
Cheenu coming towards her. She got up
from her chair. She walked over to
Cheenu and gave him a big bear hug.
Cheenu melts into that embrace. It has
been more than a month since he has
been in physical contact with any other
human being. It felt good. Cheenu and
Hema raise their heads at the same time.
Hema leads him over to the chair and the
prison warden stays at a discrete distance.
Hema holds Cheenu's handcuffed hands.
'How are you? Cheenu replied, "I am
good. When did you come back?"

Hema replied, "Only last week. I went looking for you. Your room mates told me that you were here. John organized for me to come and visit. Cheenu, why did you do this?" Cheenu started roaring his head off with laughter. Hema looked at him very perplexed. Cheenu suppresses his laughter with difficulty "Sorry Hema, I was not expecting that question from you. No one has asked me that yet. You know what? Now that you have asked me I think that I actually don't want to answer anymore. I think I was hoping to obtain understanding and emotional release but now I know that I will not get any release from any one questioning me."

Hema asked him not to be angry. "I had come looking for you to begin a life with you." Cheenu sneers, "Well Hema that was in another lifetime. You better go now. I do not want you or me to be pulled into an emotional upheaval. I just want to concentrate on the case. You can make a life with someone else. What about your mother? Is she okay now?"

Hema speaks softly. "She is settling. Her journey to healing was very difficult. That is why it took me this much time to come back. I wanted to make sure that she was definitely happy without me. Otherwise we would have just gone around in circles. Cheenu jeered, "Well, you can't expect me to know how long do you?" Hema was in pain. She was stung by his remarks "Cheenu, why are you being so cruel? Are you trying to tell me that this is all my fault?"

Cheenu shouts, "Who do you think is at fault here? You left without thinking about me. I became so lonely. Everyone else had families. I could not butt into their lives as and whenever it pleased me. If you had not gone off to help your mother, I would have been less lonely. You did not even give me your contact number when you left. You terminated all contact. It was as if you could not wait to leave."

Hema was nearly in tears. "Cheenu, you have got it all wrong. I was unsure about my feelings towards you at the time. I thought if I go away for a while, I will know better. I did not see any commitment from you either so I wanted to give you space. My mother needed me as well." Cheenu was sarcastic, "Yes go back to your mother. You can forget about me."

Hema could not sit there any longer taking his insults. She was ready to burst into tears. She just got up from her chair and walked away without looking back. If she had looked back, Cheenu would have seen the ocean of tears that had welled up in her eyes. Would Cheenu have really seen it though? He was absorbed in self pity.

Hema could not control herself. She could not stop crying all the way on the bus journey to her apartment. Thank God, she was sitting on the top floor and no one else was there. She had come with high hopes to London. She had not known about any of this. She was in shock when she heard about this from his friends. The emotion of distaste that the faces carried when they spoke about Cheenu was unbelievable. They looked at her as if they did not understand why she was asking about him. "She was playing with fire." She could see the warning in their eyes. Yet she pursued. The only people she did not visit was Priya and Venkat. She did not know them. She wanted to see Cheenu before she went and saw them.

She wanted to go and beg for forgiveness for Cheenu. Beg for their mercy to spare his life. The writing is on the wall now. She cannot ignore it any further. She will not stop loving Cheenu. The love had germinated in her heart even before she left for home. She was nurturing it and it became larger than her own being. That is how she was able to ignore his friends taunts and disdainful looks. Her mother, despite her own misery could see it. Time and again she had hinted at it. But Hema did not divulge anything. Just as well.

Hopefully time will heal her. It has to. Time is a great healer. At the moment it felt like a lot of cliche. But in actual fact that was the only truth. Time dulls the pain. She rocked herself in sync with the movement of the bus. She is supposed to get down at the depot. She has plenty of time to console herself. She will not go and see Venkat and Priya anymore. There was no point.

The two weeks flew by in the wink of an eye. Today they were going to the Crown court for the hearing. Their baby and their mother will be subject of debate in the Court today. Time and again their names will be brought up. The Public Prosecutor had warned them of that. He had coached them in what to say and what to do. He had told them to not look at Cheenu in the eye. That is all what Venkat wanted to do. Look him in the eye and ask him? Ask him how he could destroy their life. Kill his precious baby daughter. How could he hurt and kill the woman who was equal to his mother?

When people commit crimes they do it to people who are not known to them. Even professional killers think twice about hurting the people they know. They are even more protective about their family. Cheenu was not a professional killer. How did he not stop to think before even touching them?

There were many details that were not disclosed to them. Prosecution was worried that the defense will get wind of it. They travelled by a taxi to the Inner London Crown Court. The prosecutor had advised them against coming in their own car. There would be media waiting for them at the car park. Alfred did not want them to be bombarded with questions. If they came by taxi, he would be able to steer them away from the clutches of the media and bring them in safely. After the trial, they will be too emotional to drive home safely.

THE HEARING

Venkat and Priya arrived at the court in good time. Alfred was waiting for them at the curb. He quickly steered them away from the throngs of people who were waiting outside. They came together in droves. People from various nationalities, ethnic group and religion came to witness this trial. Murder was not tolerated in any of the religions. There was an emotion of anticipation and anger in the air. People were not sure if they would be allowed in. Only the presiding judge will decide and they will not hear anything until the attorney's have conferred with the judge this morning. It did not look like these people will be happy if they were turned away. The jury's were summoned a week ago and were supposed to appear in court today. The jury keeper will allocate them to different cases by randomly calling out panel members. They looked like they were already here. Some acknowledged each other, some actually smiled.

Strangers Inside

There was a sadness about the guy who was in prosthetics. His left leg was amputated. He was a retired celebrated military man. He had lost his son to the war in the Middle East as well.

The other person who was sitting and chatting to him was a retired school teacher. He was a teacher of great reputation. The ex-Prime Minister was his ex-student in school.

The man in his early thirties was a model. You could determine that by the way he kept admiring himself and how his hands always kept touching his hair.

The charity worker was a young woman twenty-five years of age. She worked for OXFAM UK. She is going to miss working with the volunteers today.

The farmer felt lost in the court surroundings. He did not know what he was going to do about his farm animals. His neighbour had promised to feed the animals and care for them. He had also employed a young man from the village to care for the land till he got back. Two weeks is a very long time in a farmer's working life. And it seems longer when he is waiting for everything to germinate, grow and turn green and lush. Well,! He could not complain. He had a lot to be thankful for.

The human rights activist probably understood that. She was trying to keep him engaged. He still looked unsure. She was a woman in her mid thirties.

That guy in the far corner was a fisherman. The way he was squinting his eyes and his weatherbeaten hands were a testimony to a difficult job.

The plumber was in a hoodie that carried his company logo. It seemed that he could not wait to get back to his work. He will lose today's tips and commissions. Of course his company will pay him the day's wages but the loss of earnings from the tips will be substantial. Any citizen could be called for Jury duty any day. At least his duty will be done.

A retired political activist was reading the newspaper. He was trying to keep himself informed.

The retired police officer kept chewing on his cigar. He was used to the court and it's functions.

A young man was skimming through a magazine. He was a regular guy who did regular jobs. He was in his early twenties

The Mental Health Doctor could read him like a book. She could see that he was bored being here. Not even a day had passed. He will be fine once the trial begins. They did not know what case they were being summoned for. Walking in blind and knowing that someone's fate rests in your hands is frightening.

The retired advocate had a group of them around him. He was explaining the in's and out's of the Jury duty to those who were interested. He did not look like a pompous man despite his profession and his reputation.

The scientist was reading a science fiction. You could see that he had no time for it. His lips were curling in disdain at every word that he read. Authors go to great lengths to get the correct information on which to base their story. Sometimes lack of critical thinking does not allow them to see if they are writing something wrong. It looked like this science fiction book had plenty of scientific mistakes!!

The lady in the corner was constantly on the phone to someone on the other end. From the conversation you could understand that she had two young children. The whole commotion on the phone was about getting them ready to go to school.

Both the public prosecutor and the defense lawyer had done well to get these people in the Jury. There was a good mix of people. It would be difficult to come to a decision regardless of whose case they are called for. The jury keeper came towards them and motioned them to gather around. All of them except for the advocate and the Military man gathered around eagerly as if he was the pied piper of Hamilton. The jury keeper asked everyone to show their panel numbers. He just wanted to ensure that they all had it on their person if they were asked to show it.

Priya and Venkat were waiting in the witness waiting room. Time lay heavy on their hands. They had read through their notes at-least a thousand times. Whatever was written on the sheet of paper did not equal the feelings in their heart and mind. They were screaming in agony and pain. All the frustration of the day had come back to them again. It was not that they had forgotten. Now they were forced to go through it again. This was an opportunity to examine their feelings about the whole incident. They had no doubts. Cheenu needed to be punished.

The same emotion echoed through the people who were waiting outside. The media had opened the case to public opinion now. They could now, because the jury were in the court house and had no access to media or news. The lady reporter from the television channel shoved the microphone into the face of the first person she could access. "Hello there, what is your opinion of the double murder case?"

This person was nervous like a rabbit caught in the headlights. She stuttered in apprehension. "Well, he should be punished. It's a pity that there is no death sentence in this country." She escaped as soon as she could. Later only, she would realise that she had her two minutes of fame. The reporter turned back to the next person. 'Sir, what do you think?

The man was self assured, "We don't know much do we? Apart from the fact that he killed two people? Regardless of the motive, killing is an inexcusable crime. We have moved away from capital punishment and I totally agree. Two wrongs do not make one right." The reporter turned to the camera, "Dear viewers, we are at the court house for the hearing of the double murder case. The public near the court house are all very angry at the accused. They are waiting anxiously for the trial to begin ......"

Hema heard this conversation as she was walking to the court room. Despite everything, she felt that she needed to be here. She had heard that Judge Treacy had agreed for spectators to enter the courtroom. She wanted to get a corner seat so she would not attract the attention of the people she knew. She went to the upstairs spectators gallery and occupied a seat that was discrete and yet allowed her to view the proceedings of the court. She could see Cheenu sitting at the defendant table. He looked handsome in a charcoal suit, a navy blazer and a dark blue tie on a light bluish grey shirt. He had his head down. Was it remorse? Or was it a feeling of detachment. What was he thinking?

Cheenu was remembering John's words. On no account was he supposed to look at the jury or the witnesses. He looked around the court room. The Jury were seated in their seats to the side. The witness box was on the opposite side of the Jury stand. The typist was sitting in front of the witness box facing the Jury. This meant that the court clerk and the Judge were to his right and the prosecutor and defendant lawyer were seated on his left. There was a television monitor in front of the jury. Cheenu was seated behind John. He could see some of the mutual friends when he entered the court house to the slogans of " baby killer down, down," ' double murderer, down, down". The world had always been against him.

He did not see Venkat or Priya. Did they not want to come? Cheenu laughed at himself. Definitely they will come. Nothing would give them more pleasure than seeing him be punished. John heard Cheenu snigger. He turned around sharply to stare at Cheenu. Before he could say anything, the Usher called out "All Rise." Everyone responded to that command automatically. Judge Treacy sailed in to the courtroom in full glory in her red robe, shoulder length wig and a white collar band. She was wearing a black skirt under the robe. She looked around the courtroom as if a king would inspect the presence of his courtiers. She loved the anticipation on the people's faces as to when she will sit down and conduct the proceedings of the court. She sat down on the high chair which was her official seat. The Usher cried out "All sit". The crowd sat down with a lot of shuffling of the feet. Judge Treacy banged the Gavel. There was pin drop silence in the courtroom.

Judge Treacy looked at Cheenu. "Defendant, are you ready to stand trial?" Cheenu bowed at the judge, "Yes My Lady" Judge looked at him through her glasses, "Good". Judge Treacy then looked at the Usher. The usher bowed and went out. He approached the jurors who were waiting next to the Court room door.

The jurors were called in by their panel numbers. One by one, the jurors came in and took their seat. The mental health doctor, the political activist, the mother of two, the retired military officer, the retired police officer, the retired school teacher, the lay person, the retired judge, the charity worker, the human rights activists, the farmer and the Scientist.

The judge looked at both the Prosecutor and the defense lawyer. 'Counsel, do you have any objections to the Jury selection?' Alfred stood up, "No my Lady". John also mumbled, "No my Lady."

Strangers Inside

The judge turned to the jurors and scrutinised them one by one and began to speak in a very authoritative voice. "Ladies and Gentlemen, thank you for giving up your precious time to discharge your jury duty. There are a few rules and regulations that you need to follow from now on.

'These are the rules'. She looked carefully at each face to check if they were paying attention.

Decide the facts of the case only.

Take directions relating to law from me the Trial Judge, whether or not you agree with me.

Remain impartial and independent. Do not look at anyone in the eye in the court room unless they address you directly.

Remain uninfluenced by any person. It is an offense for any person who is not a member of the jury to attempt to influence a juror in any way. If any person speaks to you about the case, you should inform the court or a member of the Jury-keeper.

Keep statements made in the jury room confidential. Jurors should not discuss the case with any person other than members of the jury. It is contempt of court punishable by fine and/or imprisonment to repeat any statements made in the jury room.

"Is everyone clear on that?" There was a chorus of yeses. "Now" continued the Judge, looking at the Mental health Doctor. "Juror number 1-you are the foreperson for this team of jurors. You will be the only person making any comments when questioned about the opinion of the Jury. Is that understood?"

Mental Health Doctor replied subserviently, "Yes, My Lady." Judge Treacy continued to the entire group. "The Clerk will swear you all in and the

Jury Keepers will take their oath as well."
The Court Clerk moved forward to get
the Oath and Affirmation as chosen by
the Jurors and the Jury-keepers. Then the
Usher called out "All sworn in." Judge
Tracy now looked at Alfred, the Public
Prosecutor "Counsel you may proceed".

Alfred got up from his seat. He bowed to
the judge and then turned towards the
Jury. "Respected foreperson, ladies and
gentlemen of the esteemed Jury, the
prosecution today puts forward the case
of late Mrs. Nayagam aged 65 years from
a different nationality who had travelled
to this country to be present for the birth
of her grandchild who was due to be
born soon". A photo of Mrs Nayagam
appeared on the monitor in front of the
jury. She was a graceful old woman who
looked like everyones mother with all her
jewellery, vermillion on her forehead and
adornment of flowers in her hair. A few
more photos appeared on the screen of
her in different locations in London. The
Public Prosecutor continued "Mrs.
Nayagam had travelled to London from

India to be present for her granddaughter's birth and then to stay for a while to help with childcare. This lady, who had never stepped outside of her country until she was forced by family circumstances to travel overseas was an innocent person who had a language barrier. She was a lonely person in this country. The only company she had; was of her granddaughter, daughter, her son-in-law and a handful of their friends. This woman who did everything in her power to help her daughter was rendered powerless to save her grandchild from the person who was regarded as their family friend. This is also the case of late baby Aishwarya who was abducted along with her grandmother by the man who is in the defendant box."

Baby Aishwarya's picture was displayed on the monitor. This picture was from the day of her naming ceremony. A few other pictures of a smiling, tearful, pouting Aishwarya was also displayed on the monitor. She came alive through these pictures for the people who were present in the court. She became real to the people who saw her pictures. Alfred continued "Baby Aishwarya was a beautiful child who was the apple of the eyes of her family. She was set to live life to the fullest until one day she was wiped off the face of the Earth. The charges brought against the convict are : One count of false imprisonment, one count of abduction of a minor, two counts of battery and assault and two counts of first degree murder. Dear members of the jury we advise you to watch the proceedings of the court and come to a careful conclusion of this man's guilt."

Alfred then turned to the judge. "My lady, may I ask Mrs. Priya Venkat to take the witness stand please?" Judge Tracy replied, "You may proceed Counsel." The Usher walked out to the court room door and called for Mrs. Priya Venkat. Priya arrived to the witness stand. She is sad, nervous and has lost a lot of weight. The court clerk swears her in and then Alfred approaches the witness box. "Mrs.

Priya Venkat, please tell us about your mother."

Priya looks at the judge. "My mother was a very gentle soul. She had come for my delivery and opted to stay back to bring up our baby because we both were working." Alfred coaxed her: Can you please tell us a little bit about her daily life. A sob escaped from Priya unwittingly. "No. I am sorry. I am very emotional...."

Alfred spared her the agony. "Thank you Mrs. Priya Venkat, you may leave now." Alfred to the judge, "My Lady, may I ask Mr. Venkat to approach the witness box please?" Judge Treacy looked straight at Alfred, "You may do so Counsel." The Usher went out and came back with Venkat. Once he entered the witness stand, the court clerk swore him in.

Alfred asked him, "Tell us about your daughter Mr. Venkat."

Venkat looked at the judge. His throat was wet. "My daughter was curious about everything around her. She was very attached to her grandmother. She was the only grand daughter in our family after five grandsons. The family were waiting eagerly to see her......" Venkat is unable to continue further. He stops speaking. Alfred gently asked Venkat, "How do you know this person who is sitting on the defendant's position. Please look at the judge to give your answer."

Venkat was more resolute now, "My Lady, Cheenu and me have worked in the same company for a few years now. Myself and my wife Priya treated him as a family member ....Even my mother-in-law treated him just like a son. I invited him to my house, treated him as part of my family. That is the culture in our country. We could not believe it when we heard that Cheenu was suspected in their death." Alfred thanked him, "Thank you Mr. Venkat. You may leave now."Alfred turned to the jury. "My Lady! Ladies and gentlemen, Mr. Venkat was kind to Mr. Cheenu. He offered him his friendship and he welcomed him to his house. Mr. Cheenu repaid him by killing his mother-in-law and his daughter. What kind of a person will do that? My lady, may I request to call the police Constable Imelda to the witness stand please?" Judge Treacy nodded her head.

The usher went out and escorted Imelda to the witness stand. After being sworn in, Imelda looked at Alfred. Alfred asked her, "Police constable Imelda, could you please tell me what happened on the day before you knew Aishwarya and her granny were kidnapped". PC Imelda replied, "My Lady, myself and police Constable Mathew were patrolling the area when we saw Mrs. Priya Venkat collapse outside her door. We rushed to her aid after calling for help. There was a ransom note in her hand. We escorted her to her living room, provided first aid and called for additional help."

A bomb explosion occurred inside Cheenu's brain. Venkat had not approached the police! What had he done? He had assumed Venkat to have gone to the police. That is why he got so annoyed and hasty. He got angry enough to kill them both. "Oh my God! He can never be forgiven." He came out of his reverie when the Judge banged the gavel. Just like him the spectators were flabbergasted. They were also not aware that the couple had not gone to the police of their own accord.

PC Imelda continued, "Venkat was already on his way home and reached their home just as Mrs. Priya Venkat had regained consciousness. He was horrified that someone had kidnapped them both. The minute he read the contents of the note, he asked us to leave." Alfred asked, "Did you leave?"

PC Imelda replied carefully. "No, Usually it takes 24 hours to establish that someone has been kidnapped and not missing of their own accord. But we had a ransom note that confirmed that there were two kidnappings, one that of a small baby. As per the law, we were duty bound to act immediately." Alfred asked, "What was Venkat's attitude to your involvement?"

PC Imelda replied, "He was actually torn. He did not want any harm befall them because of our involvement but he also did not have any other choice than letting us stay and getting on with the job. He could not have gone to anyone else. He could not trust anyone anymore."

Alfred finished with Imelda, "Thank you Officer." He turned to the judge, "My Lady, may I ask Jim to approach the bench?" Judge Tracy nodded. Jim was sworn in. Alfred to Jim, "Could you please tell us your full name?" Jim replied, "Jim, Sorry! James Caldwell" Alfred asked him, "What did you see on the morning of the10/11/2017?"

Jim answered, "I am a homeless man. I usually occupy the warehouse for the night and go begging during the day. Two weeks before that day, I was taken ill and taken to hospital. I had to stay there for two weeks. When I came back, I thought that the warehouse was not the way I had left it. But it belonged to someone else so I thought that may be the owner had come back. I went inside to keep my stuff and I found two dead bodies there. I immediately called the police." A picture of Mrs Nayagam and Aishwarya's dead body loomed up on the screen. A collective gasp arose from the spectators.

Alfred waited for the dramatic effect to subside. Judge Treacy banged her gavel once again. "Silence please. Next time anyone gasps in my court, I am going to throw them out." Alfred asked Jim, "Was this the dead body that you saw?"

Hema could not believe what she was seeing. She did not feel involved so far but after seeing the picture of their dead bodies she could not help herself from hating Cheenu. "What had he done? Oh the poor mite! He took their lives without a reason". Tears streamed down Hema's face. The spectator who was sitting beside her gave her an awkward look. Hema wiped her tears and returned her attention to the trial. Jim confirmed, "Yes this was the dead body I saw".

Alfred now asked the judge, "May I ask detective Dev to take the stand please?" Detective Dev walked to the witness stand and took his oath. When Dev was sworn in, Alfred asked him, "Detective Dev, could you please tell us how you came to the conclusion that Mr. Cheenu was the perpetrator?" Detective Dev replied, "My assistant Brenda, myself and my team questioned all the people known to Venkat and his family. Based on the short form of Venkat's name that was used in the ransom note, we decided that there are only four people that we needed to target. We out-ruled three of them and eventually we arrested Cheenu and took

DNA evidence. We matched it with the syringe that we found at the murder site. It was a perfect match. Cheenu then confessed in the presence of his lawyer to the crime." Alfred said to the judge: "With this I rest my case my Lady."

John got up from his chair and addressed the Jury. "Ladies and gentlemen, please look at Mr. Cheenu. Look how innocent he is? Does he look capable of murder? He is a young man who goes about his job and is a respectable member of society. He pays his taxes. He is entitled to the same case of reasonable doubt as much as we are. I am going to call a witness to prove to you that Mr. Cheenu cannot have killed Mrs Nayagam and baby Aishwarya under normal circumstances.

John turned to the judge, "My Lady, may I have permission to call Cheenu's Manager? Judge Tracy said, "Go ahead Counsel." Cheenu's manager entered the witness stand and took the oath. John approached the stand. John asked Mr. Wilkins when he was sworn in "How do you know this person, Mr. Wilkins?"

Wilkins answered, "He is an employee in the Company ECC Ltd. I am his manager." John asked him, "What is the quality of his performance at work?" Wilkins reported, "He works hard. He completes his projects on time. He is never late coming in but..." John encouraged him, "But what Mr. Wilkins?" Wilkins replied, "He becomes agitated and irritated after five O' clock. He refuses to stay over and complete a job."

John asked him: "Does he show any physical sign of agitation?" Wilkins replied, "Yes he looks at the clock again and again from 1630 onwards. He begins to tremble by 1645. At 1700 he is very annoyed and irritated. If he does not leave by 1705 he begins to give out to every one." John asked him, "Did you not think of expelling him from the job?"

Wilkins replied, "No he is a good worker. No employee has to stay after 5 pm by force. We have to pay them overtime if they stay over. They stay over by choice and are recompensed appropriately. If we expelled Cheenu, he could have gone to the court on grounds of unfair dismissal. So he was not doing anything wrong." John was happy with the response, "Thank you Mr. Wilkins."

He then turned to the judge and asked permission for the prison warden to take the stand. The prison warden takes the stand and takes the oath in willingness to testify. John asks the warden, "Officer could you tell us about Mr. Cheenu when he was a guest of her majesty, the queen?"

Prison Warden said that Cheenu was a model prisoner until five p m in the evening. He then begins to act like a demon. "It was as if a monster had taken over his body and soul." John asked, "How did you cope with that?"

Prison Warden replied, "With the court's permission, we got the prison psychiatrist to assess Cheenu. He asked us to provide Cheenu with poker cards. Cheenu was much more reasonable after he got the poker cards. John to the prison warden, "Thank you officer, you may leave the stand now." John turned to the judge, "My Lady, I am going to ask Dr. Ferdinand, the prison psychiatrist to approach the witness box please." John turns towards Dr. Ferdinand after he was sworn in.

John asked Dr. Ferdinand. "Doctor, you assessed Cheenu in prison. What is the conclusion you arrived at?" Dr. Ferdinand replied, "I assessed Cheenu on the order of the court. I found that Cheenu has addiction towards gambling." John asked, "Can people get addicted to gambling?"

Dr. Ferdinand, "Yes they can. If they have low self esteem, if they are lonely, stressed or for various other reasons."

John asked Dr. Ferdinand, For the benefit of the people in the court, may I ask you, "What is addiction?"

Dr. Ferdinand supplied the information, "Addiction is a psychological issue. Any person like you or me can get addicted to a substance or behaviour. Addiction is usually an unhealthy focus on pursuing the substance/behaviour, excluding other activities that aren't related to using the substance or behaviour. Going out of the way mainly to use this behaviour, needing more of the substance/behaviour to get the same feeling of elations and neglecting other areas of life including relationships, health, or career."

John further asked, "Could you call the addictive behaviour as insanity?" Dr. Ferdinand replied, "Yes addiction is a psychological issue and people can go to any length to fulfil their desire. Cheenu also had drugs in his system. Combined with his desperate need for money and the effect of drug will have driven

Clive Dev

Cheenu to the verge of insanity and murder." John further persisted, "Dr. Ferdinand, can you confirm that Cheenu is insane?"

Dr. Ferdinand replied, "Yes, based on my up to date knowledge and years of practice experience, I can confirm that Cheenu is psychologically disturbed. He can be cured of his addiction if he commits himself to a psychiatric institution. The court can also order the treatment." John turns around to the jury: Ladies and gentlemen, as you heard Dr. Ferdinand say that Cheenu is insane. He did not carry out the kidnap and the murder in the right frame of mind so he deserves to be acquitted. Turning to the judge John, "My Lady, with this, I rest my case".

Judge Tracy looked at the Jury box. "Can the foreperson stand up?" The mental health doctor stood up. Judge Tracy looked directly at the doctor "You and your team of jurors have a huge task.

There are a few questions to which you have to decide without any bias. You have heard the argument in the court for the last six hours. Retire to your holding cell and come to a conclusion on the following points:

Is Cheenu guilty of false imprisonment?

Is Cheenu guilty of abduction of a small child?

Is Cheenu guilty of double manslaughter?

Can Cheenu be acquitted on grounds of insanity?

You have to come back with your answer after lunch.

The Usher cried, "All rise." Everyone got up to their feet. Judge Treacy got up and moved out to her chambers. The prison officer escorted Cheenu out to the door. On the way out of the court room, he saw Venkat and Priya standing on the corridor. Something broke inside Cheenu. It was as if the whole tableau of the court argument spun around him in slow motion.

'We were patrolling the area...... We saw Mrs. Priya Venkat collapse.... We rushed to her aid......." "We were patrolling the area...... We saw Mrs. Priya Venkat collapse.... We rushed to her aid......." "We were patrolling the area...... We saw Mrs. Priya Venkat collapse.... We rushed to her aid......."

Cheenu screamed in frustration. At the same time, Cheenu pulled out the gun from the escorting prison officer's holster. The officer turned back in alarm. He was astounded. Everyone looked at Cheenu in alarm. Everyone raised their arms in surrender. The prison officer tried to reach out to snatch his gun back.

Cheenu warned, "No stand back. If anyone comes near me......". Everyone moved slowly back to their original position..... Venkat and Priya are shocked. Cheenu looks pitifully at Venkat and Priya.

Cheenu whined, "Venkat, I am really sorry. I did not know that the police got involved without your wish. I was angry at you for calling them. That is why I killed your mother and daughter. I am sorry. I don't deserve forgiveness."

Cheenu bends over as if he is in pain. A gun shot is heard. The media reporter turns back and sees Cheenu lying on the floor with blood gushing out of his neck. His eyes are staring at the horizon. Dev, Brenda, Alfred, John, Priya and Venkat are in shock.

Venkat and Priya are horrified. They wanted justice for their daughter and mother. They did not wish for him to die. They did not ask for any of this to happen. They would rather have their daughter and mother back. But we always do not get what we ask for.

Whether Cheenu deserved to die or not, he destroyed a few lives in the process. The family of the deceased, his solicitor who tried his level best to save him, the prison officer whose career record he spoiled by pulling out his gun, his friend Hema who had hoped for a chance at a life with him but more importantly his own mother. He denied her a chance to see her only son alive one more time. Cheenu stayed true to himself alone. He remained selfish to the very end.....

Life is so uncertain. People can be so unpredictable. You don't know where the stranger is. May be your neighbour, your colleague, your friends. Anyone near you or it could even be you !!!!!!

There can be a stranger inside or a stranger enside you.

FILM STORIES COLLECTION

We are a team of story/script writers of different genre focused on Book Publication and film production. Some are the Glimpses / Narratives of our creations. Our projects are subject to intellectual copy right. If you like our Narratives and if you are interested in film production.

Please Visit :
clivestorycreations.com

Clive Dev

Leabharlanna Poiblí Chathair Baile Átha Cliath

Dublin City Public Libraries

9 781792 871337